within

Short Stories for the Evolving Multicultural Woman

Written by
Aditi Wardhan Singh

RAISING WORLD CHILDREN

Raising World Children LLC
Paperback - ISBN-13: 978-1-956870-98-5
Hardcover - ISBN-13: 978-1-956870-97-8
Library of Congress Control Number - 2022900341
Virginia, United States of America
Cover Design by - Noor Alshalabi

Thank you, Shubham, for showing me all that the world and I hold within, the good, the bad, and the funny. For pushing me to follow my dreams and for taking the kids to the park when I needed to write.

Contents

Author's Note

Girl from Nowhere. That is how I used to see myself growing up in Kuwait, as a child with an Indian heritage, displaced by war moving between cities. When I became a mother, I realized that my family and I, in fact, belong everywhere. As an immigrant, getting a job was difficult, so I spent hours at Borders (back when it existed) and Barnes and Noble and honed my passion for writing. I started writing about the challenges of multicultural families and went on to create resources for multicultural families like mine who struggle daily in various ways. Because acceptance of the world begins with ourselves.

I went from blogger (on Orkut... yeah, that's how old I am!) to freelance writer to starting RaisingWorldChildren.com to an author of nonfiction/children's books who won a few awards, got onto the Bestseller list of Amazon, and got the much-coveted Teacher's Pick honor. But one horizon was yet to be overcome.

The world of make-believe where many adults spend their time daydreaming.

These stories have been written and rewritten over a span of ten years. These are stories of you, me, or someone we may have momentarily glanced at, at the store or across the street. At different stages of life, fighting their inner demons consciously or otherwise. Stories of good people striving to be better.

They are purposely written for the busy reader

who wants a quick read with their coffee/chai. So, yes, you can read this book in any order. No, the stories are not too long. They are snippets of lives from make-believe people around the world.

If you have read any of my other work or not, know that it strives to find that balance between the many worlds we currently inhabit. mindfully. The old and the new along the many borders that we touch. These stories do the same. In a world that strives to be politically correct and non-offensive, being a creator is a dangerous gig. So, please read the coming stories with an open heart.

Per acknowledgements, I want to thank Minali Bajaj Syed, who took over as managing editor of RWC, which opened up my time to work on this dream. A special note to Noor Alshalabi, who brought my vision for the cover and the actual book alive. The multiple editors who worked with me patiently on this book with their feedback, who I am going to blame should anyone have issues with the book! And, of course, my friends, family, and children that support my writing endeavors.

If you wish to, feel free to connect via **contact @raisingworldchildren.com.** I love hearing from readers.

Thank you for picking up this book. You will never know how much it means to me that you chose my work to spend your most precious commodity on—time. **I request you to give me a few more moments to leave a kind review on Amazon, so others may be encouraged to read this book as well.**

बुरा जो देखन मैं चला, बुरा न मिलिया कोय ।
जो दिल खोजा आपना, मुझसे बुरा न कोय ।।

The wrong I went looking for,
No wrong did I see

When I searched within, there was
No One as wrong as me

– Kabir Das (Indian Poet)

"Everyone thinks of changing the world, but no one thinks of changing himself."

– Leo Tolstoy (Russian Writer)

Within

prejudice

The colorful marigolds and roses on and around the mandap looked magical. The white gazebo was the perfect setting for the holy matrimony.

The bride's crimson lehenga with traditional embroidery and gota patti on her dupatta looked just perfect. These days, kids wore whatever color they liked, but shades of red just spoke at weddings. The groom looked lovely in his cream shervani with matching crimson embroidery.

Devika scrolled through the photos of the wedding with a smile on her face, remembering the festivities with fondness. She hummed the banna banni song she had sung at the sangeet. Everyone had been so surprised she still remembered so many folk songs. The young so often underestimate the old.

The sangeet. The jai mala. The couple dancing. The bride's entry with the sunglasses, dancing with her brothers holding the dupatta over her head. These days everyone does their own take on traditional customs. Gone are the days of the demure bride. Devika wished she had enjoyed her own wedding as much. In those days, you just sat in the corner, eyes downcast while everyone around you had a blast at your father's expense.

The photoshoot of the couple just before the reception was wonderful. She hadn't seen these pictures before, probably because the couple's team uploaded them directly to Instagram.

Her eyes slipped to the comments in curiosity. So many congratulatory messages from fellow actors and colleagues. She beamed with pride, and then, like a bright red burning flame, were the snarky comments.

"Why in the world did she marry this monkey?"

"Kallu mama! Her fairness is needed to help him see himself."

"Her ex was so dashing. Dey looked so much btr 2gether."

"These people. Aaj woh kal koi aur. Flitting from one guy to another.

...

"Chi Chi. Keede lagein. What is wrong with these people? Badtameez. Scoundrels." Devika couldn't stop scrolling and reading each comment.

"What happened, Nani?" Her sixteen-year-old granddaughter Jeeva walked into the room and snuggled up on the sofa, peering into her grandmother's phone, ignoring her own for a minute. "Oh! You should never look at those comments Nani. Bad idea."

"Arre. What did I know? People would be so mean."

"Forget it. It's not like Aunt Nutan ..."

"Nutan *masi*."

Jeeva rolled her eyes, "What difference does it make?"

"Aunt is respectful but impersonal. We say aunt for every older woman who is not related. Masi shows she is related."

"Who am I showing?" Jeeva raises her shoulders and hands, looking around. "Either way, she will still be mom's cousin, na?"

"Haan, but Masi is better than aunt or calling by name. More affectionate also." Nani pursed her lips, giving the final word. "And how many times have I told you to wear longer shorts when we are having guests over. Can't make out you are wearing anything under."

Jeeva ignores the last comment and emphasizes her use of the word, "Nutan *masi* is too famous to bother with these dumb opinions. These trolls just have nothing better to do than stalk people online and talk about that which they have no idea about. Thanks to fake news." She adds air quotes.

“Par aise kaise they say these things. See. Bad words also.” Devika raised the phone higher to show Jeeva.

“Haan toh, you look at the good comments, na. Those are so much more. Aap woh chod do. Don’t fret about these.”

“Makes me sad. How can they say such things? The boy and girl love each other. Inko kya padi hai. It’s none of their business na, who she marries.”

Pavitra walked into the room, adjusting her Bandhani sari, walking to the cupboard to pick out her jewelry. She addresses her question to Jeeva. “Kya hua? What’s mom upset about?”
“Nani is upset with the trolls on Nutan masi’s profile.”

Pavitra smiled at Jeeva’s use of Masi, happy that her daughter made the effort and said, “That’s the world we live in now. Besides, Nutan picked the life of an actress. When you put yourself out there, this is bound to happen. Especially people on social media these days, who follow their life. They take things personally because they feel attached to these mirages and pedestals that they create. You won’t believe the memes people our own family are forwarding on the WhatsApp group the whole family is on. Saying they are funny. They don't realize how she will feel when she sees them."

Nani made a face as if she had eaten a lemon, "Jealous! Making fun to show her up. Distasteful it is. How can they write such things to someone they don't even know."

"Everyone thinks they have a right to say things about famous people, like that dhobhi wala," Jeeva quipped.

Pavitra turned around. "Who?"

"That story Nani always tells from the Ramayan when that dhobi wala lamented to Lord Ram that Sita had been with Raavan for so many years, so she must be *impure*. Then Lord Ram left her."

"Don't you remember what happened before he left her and after?" Devika smiled, happy Jeeva had remembered the story.

"Yeah, I do, Sita was forced to give that agni pareeksha, walk through fire to prove her innocence. And even after she did, Lord Ram exiled her. She raised her twin sons Luv Kush all by herself. I never understand why people pray to Lord Ram then. How can you pray to a man who leaves his wife?"

Devika places a hand on her granddaughter's. "The story doesn't stop there. After her exile, when everyone gets reunited, Sita leaves Ram forever by going back to Mother Earth. It shows a lot of things. One, when you are in the public eye, everyone thinks they can talk, but that doesn't mean you should listen. Two, if you take the opinion of others into consideration, then you could end up making bad decisions. Three, it shows that even gods can make mistakes and have to suffer consequences. Lord Ram was heartbroken when Sita ma left him. It is an age-old empowering story to learn that in our culture, women have always walked away or taken a stand for their self-respect. Be it Sita Mata in Ramayan or Draupadi in Mahabharat.

"All those stories show the good and bad sides of all humankind, man or woman or any other. Lord Ram made a mistake after a lifetime of being the perfect son, husband, brother and the many kindnesses he bestowed, even on strangers. We don't pray to these gods because they lived an ideal life. We pray because their stories show us the ways to live our life. To avoid the mistakes they made. It also shows, even the most perfect person is subject to fault."

"I didn't think of it like that." Jeeva ponders.

"Sita should have stayed with Ram and her sons," Pavitra spoke up with her back to her mom and daughter, browsing through her bangle collection. "For Nutan also, I think it's enough now, ma. She should stop acting. Actresses don't have a long shelf life anyway. And soon, it will be time to start a family. She can't travel the world with a baby in tow."

"Plus, in this social media age, all this trolling is so toxic. Imagine subjecting a child to this world. I am so happy I am not on social media. So lucky we didn't have it when we were young. It is so addictive. Trying to please all the eyes on you all the time. So exhausting. And for famous people like Nutan, the memes, the jokes people and influencers make... about her movies, her exes, the dresses she wears. What will her in-laws think!"

Devika spoke up, "That is their problem, Pavitra, not ours."

"Ma, she's had two relationships in the public eye before this marriage. It's all out there."

"So? That just makes her very sure of who she wants in her life for the long run. We introduced you to so many boys before you picked Jeeva's father to marry. In our mythological stories, women have had Swayamvars where the princesses would pick a man to marry in front of the whole courtroom. When you had the right and women had that right then, why not now? The ways are changing, but the result is the same."

"This is not the same, ma."

Devika waved her hand in front of her face, erasing the argument. "We were a civilization of highly evolved beings. Systems were developed with a lot of thought to keep things organized. Everything had a reason. But times changed, needs changed, and yet people want to hold on to archaic traditional thought while walking in the age of the internet. Ego and patriarchy made humans keep using them for their personal advantages. Beliefs are so convoluted that you cannot see right from wrong anymore.

"What someone does in their lives is no one's business but their own. If her in-laws have a problem, then they can talk to their son about it. Like I am talking to you.

"Everyone has a right to do what they want. Their life. Their choice. Unless they are being intentionally hurtful or mocking. When Nutan stops working, who she dates, what she does to manage her family life. Her choice. Whether her life partner is darker, lighter, older, younger shouldn't matter. Nutan is happy. Now, that is all that matters to me. That's all that should matter to you too, to anyone. Everyone judges another, assuming that the same would never happen to their own. We should all in fact be kinder because we all have that one person who could someday face the same needless judgment. No one knows what tomorrow holds for anyone."

Pavitra turned around, staring at her mom, understanding that her mother was talking about Jeeva. Nani put a hand around her granddaughter and pulled her close, wagging her free hand's finger at her daughter. "Besides, you say you are not on social media. But you are always on your phone, always knowing the latest gossip. Don't think I don't know how much time you spend on it. Spying on Jeeva's account too."

Jeeva smirked, and Nani nudged her. Pavitra pursed her lips in a pout.

Nani said softly, "We should always look inwards. I, in fact, like that Nutan has always done her own thing and been open about who she likes or doesn't like. It's not easy, the field she is in, and only a few make it to the top. If we, her family, only don't cheer for her, then how can we expect the world to be kind?

"Chalo now, go get my pastel pink saree from my closet. It's the first time the lovely bride and groom are coming to our home. I want to look my best." Nani patted Jeeva on her back, urging her to get up.

Jeeva closed her surprised mouth, hugged her grandmother, and ran out of the room.

Pavitra turned back to look at the mirror to add her bindi. She could see her mother in the reflection. Their eyes met, and her mother nodded at her, smiling. Pavitra smiled back.

grievances

I'm so mad; the words in this book are blurred. I don't know what to do. The last argument seemed endless, and it has been our third this week. Urgh!

Can I help it if I need to sleep with a blanket? I like to cozy into it and have the air conditioner way down. He was being so unreasonable! Quips like, "If you feel hot, take off the blanket!" or "Let the thermostat be at room temperature," or

"Sleep with a bedsheet instead, na." The nerve!

Dad was the exact same way with me. "Why do you need to keep the A/C facing you if all you are going to do is bury yourself into the blanket? Do you know the amount of energy you're wasting? Not to mention the electricity bill?" But his lectures fell on deaf ears as the gentle air from the ducts lulled me to sleep.

I sighed. I had so hoped that things would be different in my own home, but alas! It's not my fault that he can't keep a blanket on himself and then ends up freezing through the night. It has been a month since we've slept in the same room. Actually, we have hardly slept at all, and there seems to be no end to it. We would try sleeping, and either he or I would end up going into the main hall for the rest of the night. What a way for newlyweds to be.

But then, can you blame us? The way we sleep has been ingrained into us over the years, and a person needs to get comfy to be able to relax, right? *Right?*

The worst of it was, this stupid thing was the cause of our first official fight as husband and wife, and it has reached a stalemate. Maybe it was the sleepless nights that were adding fuel to the fire, but it was getting me very worried. If a stupid matter like this could have us fighting like cats and dogs, then what hope do we have for the important issues? Already I was calling him mean and unreasonable, and he was calling me pampered and stubborn. Tears burn my eyes as I recall the ugliness of the argument and imagine us arguing our way to divorce once the important matters reared their heads.

Sure, In the beginning, it was all roses and chocolates, but that's normal for any couple, right?

It's hot and heavy in the beginning and starts cooling down as time elapses. Here it was the complete opposite, metaphorically speaking. The wedding was in December, and the five months since had been cool, and now that summer had hit in full force, it seemed to be heating things up in more ways than one.

The forces of nature actually felt like they were plotting to drive us apart.

I kept forgetting to keep the bottles of water in the fridge, and he wanted a cool drink as soon as he entered the house. When we went out, I'd clamor for ice cream and golas, whereas he'd warn me about calorie intake and brain freeze.

He loves sleeping on the balcony, enjoying the natural winds, and I can't ever imagine doing that. I prefer staying indoors, and he talks about going for long walks to soak in the sun. I get cranky once I start sweating, and he revels in the vitamin D. The list goes on and on, leading to futile bickering.

Marriage is hard, *yaar*. Living with a guy for the first time seems to be about discovering things about myself as much as him. Things that seemed like natural, everyday habits have turned into things only unique to me. Adjusting to each other's life, convincing each other to try a new way of doing things seems to have become a 24/7 job.

Okay, okay. I am exaggerating quite a lot. It isn't all bad.

We can talk for hours about anything and love making each other laugh. It's been amazing to be setting up my own house, living the way I'd always imagined, and he was as much a sport at trying new things as I was, and well, to be honest, until now, the experience has been highly pleasant. In fact, I've found myself loving him more with each passing day. Yet these last few days have had me homesick, craving my comfort zone—the room I grew up in, my bed.

To be fair, he probably feels the same way. It occurred to me he was surely as miserable as me. I mean, who likes fighting, right? A sob escapes me as I think about how horrible he must think I am. He is probably sorry to have married me and is thinking of all the other girls who would have been a better match. He's probably regretting he ever...

The doorbell rings. I wipe my tears, quickly wash my face, and rush to the door.

As I pull it open, there he stands with an even more morose expression. Poor thing! How silly of me to pester him so. He must be equally tired from lack of sleep. Surely, I can adjust to sleeping the way he did in time. Habits are, after all, all that we make of them.

An apology wells up from within me.

Before I can utter a word, suddenly his expression changes to one of a cute child, displaying the smile I had come to love, and out comes a rose, almost magically, from behind his back.

"I'm so sorry, sweetie," he whispers as he gives me the rose and pulls me into his arms, carrying me into the hall.

"No, no, I'm the one who should be sorry. I really didn't mean any of all that I've been saying. I've just been so tired and cranky. I guess we both have. It'll just take me some getting used to."

He pulls my hair away from my face and looks into my eyes. "You shouldn't cry over such silly things."

That only gets the tears flowing again. "It's just been so bad. Every weekend seems to be a fight fest. You must think I'm so horridly childish." I whimper.

He sets me down on his lap and beams. "Shush, now. Childish, yes, horrid? Never. I love that you bring out the child in me. It's a silly spat, and we should treat it like that. All a part of getting to know each other better. Some things we can solve, for the remaining, we will adjust over time.

"Now, what I suggest for this particularly pesky problem is we should buy you a fan. You know, one of those rotating ones that you can shift around, and then you can keep it positioned toward you. That way, you can sleep in your cozy blanket, and I can be comfy at the temperature the room is at. How does that sound?"

A giggle escapes my lips. "That sounds like another reason for me to love you. "

Those ugly problems fade away as the heat of the day increases exponentially with us kissing, all the past bitterness from the previous few days melting away...

hope

The rocking chair creaks rhythmically, a metronome in the darkness.

The sky thunders outside. She sits looking out the window. The droplets cluster on the window, colliding with each other and disappearing into nothingness.

A tear rolls down her cheek. Why would she be punished so? They were together for such a short time, but the ache of separation gripped her heart with such fierceness.

The bitterness has been eating away at her.

What had she done to deserve this? She keeps going over all their time together, wondering what she could have done differently to keep them together.

Fed him food her mom had insisted? Done the fasting for his long life?

The irony was that she hadn't even wanted him in her life. He waltzed into her world unexpectedly, and before she knew it, her every moment was about him. And now he was gone, as he had come.

Like a magician's act.

The squeals draw her attention. The neighbors' twins running in their backyard. Her mind wandered. She remembered the one time she babysat them for an hour. She had been aghast at how entitled they were. They wanted to eat everything in the house and take some for mom too.

But the way they thought, beyond their years...

She's seen the boy and girl play with each other often. How innocent and pure young relationships are. Now, they run around, jumping randomly, hoping to splash each other. Screaming in mock protest as they soak in murky waters. Their parents look from their porch indulgently. The boy pushes the girl into a puddle, and she bursts out laughing. He runs away as his parents scold him helplessly, exasperated!

She stares. Her traitorous eyes, brimming with tears. Unbeknownst to them, a smile is tugging at pale lips.

The door swings open.

"Honey! Are you okay?" He comes down to kneel beside her gazing out with her. "It'll get better. Give it time."

He caresses her knee and wraps his fingers around her limp hand. In contrast to hollow words, this simple gesture is to convey his love, their loss, their pain, his support of her.

But he will never feel what she does. Because he never felt what she did.

She touches her stomach absently.

A habit she had developed, only to be reminded again harshly that there is nothing left to caress anymore.

She looks around at the room that she had decorated with dreams of motherly love. The painted blue skies, the rainbow peeking from the clouds inside the room belie the weather outside. She had always wanted the sun to shine on her son.

Her husband squeezes again, and this time she looks at him, really looks. For days she hasn't looked at him. His face is creased with pain, his eyes red with sorrow. He, too, lost something, the possibility of a different tomorrow, someone they would have cherished together.

He, too, needs her. He, too, needs time.

The ecstatic giggling wafts back in, reminding her of another yesterday, another tomorrow. A time when they were pregnant together. A time when they may be again tomorrow.

She is grateful for him, his days and nights beside her. With a smile, she places her hand above his, letting hope envelop her.

Understanding

Rose, cherry, wine, mahogany, maroon... Different shades of red flitted below the balcony.

Looking up at the sky, hands on the railing, Shalini sighed. “It’s already nine. When will moonji come out?” Abhi cleared his throat, snickering. “Oh, sorry, *Chanda Mama.*”

Abhi wrapped his arms around her from

behind, "I don't know why you do this every year. "

"Your mom sends *sargi* every year." Shalini rolled her eyes.

"We could tell her you don't want to do it anymore."

"Oh! And be the only woman from North India who doesn't fast for her husband on Karvachauth?" Shalini shrugged.

Abhi stood up straight, looking at her. "So, you are doing this only for others? You know you don't need to do that."

Shalini realized her slip up. "No." She put her hands around his neck. "I do this cos I love you. And it's nice to have a day when I celebrate that in the moonlight." She looks up as she says this, "If only it would come out. Plus, I look amazing in red, all decked up. Hai na? "

Abhi puts his hands around her waist, pulling her closer. "That you do."

"And don't think I don't know that you haven't eaten anything all day too. Why do you fast with me?"

"You only call it Indian Valentine's Day. Toh this day is not just yours, na. It's mine too. I'll do what I can."

"You are sweet." Shalini nuzzles her head on Abhi's shoulder.

A voice called from below. "Shalini! Come and open your fast with us, na. Aa jao."

Shalini turned to look down at Pushpa aunty and smiled, nodding. "I will break fast and come down to wish everyone." Pushpa aunty waved okay, and Shalni waved back. She turned around and rolled her eyes.

"Why are you always so agro toward the building aunties!?"

"Which reason should I go with... Hmmmm..." Shalini counted off her fingers. "That they always ask when we will have kids? Or when they invite me for their themed kitty parties? Or they talk about how wonderful my life is that I get to work and enjoy outside the house while they slave inside the house. Or that they never miss a moment to mention how I have put on weight or ..”

“Woah! Catch your breath...” Abhi laughed. “They are simply from another time.”

“Yeah... they are. What about Tanuja, Vanthika and all? They are all my age and still act like stuck-up bitches. Constantly giving backhanded compliments about my clothes or our date nights or parties... As if I have gone into their homes to stop them from doing all these things.”

“Hmmm, I can imagine it’s not easy being so tied down in your head to outdated cultural norms.”

Shalini stared at him. “So you think they have a right to say those things?”

“Not at all. But we have to live in a world of such people. That is possible only if we understand where they are coming from. Yes, they are free to work outside, go for date nights, wear whatever they want, but it’s like an elephant tied to a small stick in the ground. Sure, it can run away, but it doesn’t because it doesn’t know any better.”

Shalini shakes her head unbelievingly.

Abhi took her by the shoulders, turned her around, and put his hands on the balcony railings around her. "After all, here you are. A modern girl following an age-old tradition that doesn't actually make my life long, but you do it because you are torn a little between obligation and the joys of tradition."

Shalini turned her face to stare at him.

Someone shouted, *"Chand aa gaya*. The moon has come out!"

Shalini looked down at all the colors running around. She paused, turned, and picked up her puja thali and raised her hand, yelling down, "Pushpa aunty! I am coming too..." She turned around. "Let's go see how it feels to celebrate this age-old Indian Valentine's Day with others. I am warning you, though. You start dancing; I will run!"

worth

"Who are you?"

I didn't get it at first. I was cleaning my daughter's nose with saline solution. My son came, gazed intently at his sister, and mumbled.

After three sleepless days with a six-month-old crying with cold and fever, I was distracted beyond tears. I was missing my mom and wishing I had help taking care of two sick kids.

How in the world do women do this while working a 9 to 5 job?

I was too busy trying to do what I was doing without further traumatizing a wailing child. After I was done, my son came and put a hand on my shoulder and asked again, "Who are you?" I laughed out loud.

"You don't know who I am. I'm your Mummy, right?"

He shook his head and persisted with the question, further elaborating, "Who are you? Are you a doctor?"

Ah. Cleaning his sister's nose, giving her much-needed relief during her cold and fever, made his four-year-old mind wonder.

I, of course, found it amusing and affirmed. "Yeah, I'm a doctor. I help you also when you get a boo-boo." He smiled and said, "You are a good doctor," and continued playing with his blocks.

I picked up his sister and soothed her, checking if the instant pot was done cooking the Rajma and the rice was done on the stove with my other hands. I prayed for seven o'clock to arrive soon so I could hand the kids over to their dad.

...

The next day, the question arose when I was trying to teach him to write. “Who are you? Are you a teacher?” And so on it went.

Random comments would pass while I was doing generic stuff.

“Who are you? Are you a pilot?” when I drove the car.

“Who are you? Are you a helper?” when I helped him tie his shoes.

“Who are you? Are you a worker?” when I’m looking for something on the laptop.

Reminds me of that post online where it says, I’m a mom. I do everything twenty-four by seven. But of course, my son doesn’t know how to read yet. Children and their minds.

I am cutting veggies when I remember to video call mom for her recipe for kothimbir vadi.

Mom picks up the call after endless ringing. I

can only see her nose and chin.

"Ma, please focus your face."

"Haan beta! Bolo. Kaisi hai?"

"I'm okay. How are you doing?"

"Thandi badh rahi hai. Sweater nikaal diye hain. Just waiting for dad to pull the heaters."

"I called to ask about your kothimbir vadi recipe. Can you email it to me?"

"Sure beta! How is laddoo?" Mom is distracted. She doesn't wait for an answer. "Pushpa's daughter just joined Amazon as a manager, you know. "

I cringe within. "Good for her. Tell aunty I wish her well."

"Woh baat aur hai that she doesn't have two kids."

"Hmm." I know what's coming next. She is about to go into her usual loop.

"It's good you are home for the kids now. Poor

other kids have to go to daycare, but I dream of one day when you will stand on your own two feet and earn your own money."

I sigh loudly. The baby starts crying, and I pick her up.

"Mom, those are not poor kids. They are happy at daycare with other kids, and I am standing on my own now also. "

"Haan haan, I know. But it's not the same. Other girls your age are doing so much and are so fit also. Are you going for walks? I told you, na, drink lemon water every morning to lose that baby fat. Focus on yourself. It's important."

"Acha ma, I have to go pick up Nivu from preschool now. I gotta go. Please email me the recipe, na. Yeh bol rahe the, he wants to have those during the weekend."

"Haan Haan, you go!"

The call ended. I looked at the blank screen and then at my baby cooing in my arms.

I sat on the rocking chair, nuzzling laddoo, smelling her in. This is my time with her alone.

We rock for fifteen mins, she goes to sleep. I cradle her into the car seat and drive the car to preschool.

I see Nivu waving at me from the carpool lane. “Mama!” he shouts, getting into the car. “Can we go to the park today and have McDonald’s?”

“Sure, and then grocery shopping after that, okay?”

Nivu loved going grocery shopping with me. Helped me pick stuff and asked a million questions about prices and why I picked what I chose. We met new people; he had long conversations with the strangers at the checkout line. We pick lunch and go to the park and eat together, having a relaxed and happy conversation.

“Who are you today, Mama?”

“Today, I just want to be your mama. Is that okay?

“Yup! That’s the best you.” Nivu’s eyes twinkled as he looked over the laddoo sleeping.

confidence

One day, I saw a stranger.

I was twenty-one, and she was maybe in her forties... ish.

Wearing a crisp sari, with hair tied into a tight bun and with just the right amount of makeup and jewelry, standing at the train's entrance, she was looking out at the passing world, deep in thought.

I wanted to be her someday—someone who another would look up to. She looked so confident. Her posture was so proper, holding her purse in the most elegant way.

She looked perfect.

She probably didn't need to know how perfect she was. Someone so beautiful already knew, I am sure. I was drawn to tell her. I had never complimented a stranger before.

As I stood on the other side of the entrance, the air from the rushing train running at our faces, I said, "Excuse me."

She turned around. Smiled.

"You are really elegant. I love your sari. I hope I can wear a sari like you someday."

Her smile increased ten-fold and reached her now clearly twinkling eyes.

"You will not believe the horrid day I've had. I needed to hear something like that. You really made my day! Thank you so much. You are so sweet."

And we went on talking about where we lived and what we did, only to never meet again.

Her stop was about to come. She primed to get off when she turned to say, "It takes a confident person to do what you did today, adding sparkle to another's day. Never change."

acceptance

I hate the rain. I'm wet and sticky. The dirty water has soaked through my jeans. I should have taken the umbrella when Mom suggested it, but I was being my stubborn self. Yeah, I am fully aware of this marvelous aspect of my sparkling personality.

You can't blame me. The weather forecast didn't say anything about it pouring today. I guess my mom is better at predicting the weather.

Planning a surprise party is hard enough without having to roam around drenched.

I don't know why I talked myself into making their twenty-fifth a big one. No, the truth is I know why. They are nice people. Great parents and all that jazz.

People around me seem to be equally miserable as they make a dash for it with their umbrellas held high. Good to know I'm not the only grouch. I curse myself for taking the long road home. I hate the rain. I had forgotten about the monsoons being this brutal. Two short years away from home in New York has changed me so much!

Except the desire to catch a glimpse of her. I came out at this time to book the hall, hoping to catch her below her building, maybe strike up a conversation. I'm kicking myself. There's no way she's stupid enough to be roaming around in this weather. My feet stop short, all by themselves.

I rub the water from my glasses. Is it a

mirage, or is that really Ashita, right in the middle of that empty stretch of road? Is she crazy? Twirling around in the rain, with her hands outstretched as if she's flying a plane, catching rain drops on her tongue.

No, No, No... Don't do it! And there she goes into the puddle. I wince.

Ten years of loving her—since I was sixteen—and we are still right here. Three buildings away and miles apart in the heart.

The black shirt and blue jeans look amazing on her. So simple and yet most alluring. The raindrops make her shine. She looks amazing in everything.

I shouldn't go here. But with her long, auburn hair wet the way it is and her clothes clinging to her, I know I can't stop staring. Now she realizes she's not alone in the world. The look of defiance she's giving the passers-by is hilarious. Wait! Are those tears in her eyes? Crap! I avert my eyes.

"Hey! Hi!"

She's caught me. She probably felt me staring.

People always know when they're being stared at. Should I pretend I didn't hear her? She's looking straight at me. I might as well say hi.

It would be rude not to, right? I wonder what her hair smells like. Is it different from when it's dry?

"What are you doing here? I know you hate this weather."

I see her wiping her eyes in haste. So they *were* tears I saw. I hope it's nothing serious. Man! She looks as embarrassed as I am feeling. Hell! She was the one dancing in the rain while crying. I was simply walking by, and I still feel I did something much worse, intruding on her private moment.

I stammer. "H—Hi, Ashita. I was just coming back from booking the hall. You know... for the surprise party I'm throwing my parents? You are coming, right?"

She is lost. Her expression seems vague. Did she really forget? Wow, and here I was thinking I would tell her how I felt. I always thought there was something brewing between us. Probably not if she can't even remember being invited to my parents' anniversary.

"Uh, of course." She slaps her head in exaggerated fakeness. "I'll try to be there." The way her eyes avoid me says she won't.

Silence.

I'm not going to insist. She's surely thinking up excuses of why she can't come. Might as well talk about something else. "So, enjoying the rain?" I give her my most charming smile. Well, my mom says it is, anyway.

She beams. "Yeah, it's wonderful! The smell of the earth when the first drops fall. The touch of each drop on the skin. When it rains, it feels like everything is right in the world again. Don't you think so?"

The way she talks about it, without a doubt, monsoons are the best. "Yeah, sure!"

Especially now that they are associated with a fond memory of her.

She looks beyond me over the horizon and smiles. Uh oh—that's her sad smile. Something is terribly wrong. I can't help myself as I almost reach out to touch her. "Are you okay?"

She's uncertain about her answer. Whatever comes out of her mouth next is going to be a half-truth. I've known her for over a decade now. Tutoring, chilling with neighborhood friends, and parties with parents. We would always find our own time together, discussing our days, our dreams.

"I have to leave my job and move with my parents to Bangalore when they retire. I'll be giving my notice tomorrow."

Shit! Shit! Shit. I realize my mouth is open in surprise, and I shut it. "Why?"

It's me who's the idiot. I've been waiting for the perfect occasion, to take her out for a lavish dinner and floor her with an over-the-top romantic gesture like a horse-drawn carriage ride or an orchestra or sitting by Marine Drive, our favorite spot by the water.

Damn me and my planning!

I'm screwed! Her parents have probably found the perfect guy for her, and a few months down the line, she'll be married to someone else while I'll be sitting holding the invite. Isn't that usually how it goes?

She looks sadder than before now. "Well, I guess they don't want me to live alone once they are gone. Aai Baba say it's better in Bangalore with our extended family. I'll find a job there."

A crucial piece in this answer is missing. I ignore the feeling. "But you don't have another job lined up, do you? Shouldn't you get your ducks in a row? Why don't you wait a while before you go gallivanting off to another city?" She's surprised by my tone. I sound rude in my desperation.

"We‘ve been talking about it for a few weeks now. I think it makes sense."

Her eyes glance down and then back up at me. So many questions; so few answers...

The rain is between us now, a curtain of sorts. I can see her through it, but she's not completely there. The rain drops fall on her, down her body, and into the ground. I wonder how that feels. My heart plummets. I can't let her leave, not like this. It's now or never!

I leave it to fate. Rain is supposed to be romantic as hell anyway, or so say all the Bollywood movies ever.

I grab her hand and drag her behind the building to the kids' park, where no one is around. I gesture toward the bench. She leans on the wall next to it instead. I stand in front of her. I hope she feels the same way. I hope she knows how much I mean this.

I reach out and hold her hand within mine. She doesn't pull away.

"A—Ashita, is this what you truly want? I could give you a reason to stay back here. You are everything I've ever wanted and everything I'll ever need. I knew I loved you from the moment you stepped into Mrs. Vergheese's chemistry tuition, in that white salwar kameez with that bandhani dupatta and those silver jhumkas. Every time you laugh. Every time you giggle.

Every time you succeed at anything, I want to be there to see you. I have known since then beyond any doubt that you are the person I want to try to make happy for the rest of my life. Do you think you could feel the same way about me?"

Her mouth forms the most beautiful "O" I've ever seen. It's not a yes, but she's not running away either. That's a sign, in a way.

I wait a moment. A laugh escapes. Is that a good sign? No, wait. They are joined by big, fat tears sliding down her pretty face. I don't know what that means. I'm shivering now, not from the cold, but from the words that those lips are going to utter. I have never been more scared in my whole life, and I have been skydiving!

She pulls her body off the wall. The palm of her hand touches her stomach. She takes a step back. She wipes her tears. It's the saddest I've ever seen her, and my heart breaks knowing I did that.

Okay, time for some damage control, "Hey! Hey!" I laugh out loud. "Don't cry. I'm sorry... I was just kidding. I was kidding. Can't you take a joke?" I'm making weird chuckling noises that sound horridly stupid even to my years. Of course, I wasn't kidding, but it is a way out for her.

She is amused by my retraction. "No, you were not." She sighs. God, this is going to suck, but she's honest and kind. I'm sure she'll let me down easy.

"I might as well tell you. You'll know sooner or later, and you deserve to know this from me. "

I steel myself against the onslaught of kind words dripped in pity.

"I'm sick."

Not what I expected.

"You know those stomach problems I've been having? I am sure your mom told you... Don't act surprised. My mom tells your mom everything, I know. Well, I've been going to the doctor for it, and..."

She breathes out air slowly, more to calm herself. I, on the other hand, have stopped breathing,

"It's a tumor. I need surgery, that's why my parents want me with them. They want a second opinion and want to make sure the rest of the check-ups are done with them present. I'm still waiting on the results here before they give me the details of the... you know... the treatment."

I died a million deaths at that moment.

I process and digest, thinking hard about what to do. Am I still here? I don't really know how to react. What do you say to someone in such a difficult situation? So, I do the most logical thing. I pull her to me, hugging her tightly.

She bursts into tears. She has probably been crying herself to sleep for many nights, all alone. I hope my hug is comforting to her. A hug reserved for a friend, a loved one telling you they care. I surprise myself by being this cocky. I guess I'm hoping I'll get the reaction I desire.

"Does this mean that if you weren't sick, you'd be saying yes?"

She jerks her head up, looking at me, blinking hard and fast. She's shocked by my response. I grin.

She bites her lower lip. Her limpid eyes are smiling slightly.

"I have waited for you to say something for years now." She laughs. "You do have horrible timing. Another day, another time, I'd probably be dancing in the rain because you said what I've always wanted to hear, rather than just wanting to live until I'm eighty with you, to feel connected to this world, in case..." She's crying again. "...I am not here tomorrow to feel it." She sniffles. "Gross... That sounds corny. See? You don't need this drama. No one does."

I pull her away from me by her shoulders and wipe her tears. I push her chin up a bit. "We are friends first. You just let me decide what I need. Let's get you through this first, and then we can plan our wedding date, or if you want, we can start right now. That'll have you adding many more things in that 'things to worry about' list you always keep in your purse."

When she chuckles, her eyes crinkle. I look beyond her. There's a rainbow on the horizon, in the clouds, hazy yet there. Awe-inspiring, yet pale in comparison to the strength of her soul, a soul that dances in the rain when most would be broken. I point out the rainbow to her.

"Isn't that another one of the things that make the rain special? Now, let's get you back to your apartment and out of those clothes, and then we can talk some more... Go home, get your tests done, and I can come to visit if that's okay with you." As we walk toward her apartment, I entwine my fingers into hers. I spot a puddle. Veering her toward it, I kick the water, splashing her, and she dutifully returns the courtesy.

She stops short. "What do you think our parents will say?"

"I think my mom has always known, that's why she keeps in touch with your mom throughout. What do you think your mom will say?"

She turns to look at the rainbow. "Probably that marrying a girl is not a big deal when compared to the possibility of your child dying." She shows me her tongue and chortles.

Dark humor suits her. I smile. She's radiant. Walking in the rain does feel amazing with the right person to share it with, however long it lasts.

kindness

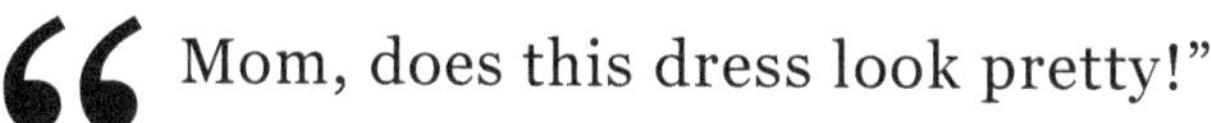

"Mom, does this dress look pretty!"

"Yes, Ellora," Sara said as she looked in the mirror, placing each sari adorned hanger against her body. The theme of the party was green, and her options were between a bottle-green chiffon with a gold border or a light-green Bandhani saree.

She placed them on the bed and picked up her

jewelry case to see what she had that would match the sarees better. That would be the deciding factor.

"Are you sure?" Ellora came in front of the mirror, looking at herself in the mirror.

Sara looked at her adorable eight-year-old daughter, looking adorable in a lime-green salwar kameez she had picked up for her during their last India trip.

"Yes, my darling!" She continued looking through her bangle collection.

"How do you know?"

Sara laughed. "Because you are the most beautiful girl in all the lands."

Ellora twirled, pleased, but paused, looking in the mirror again. She looked at her mom sideways. "Are you just saying that?"

Sara stopped her searching and looked at her daughter, with her long curly hair, sweet face, and asked, "Why do you say that?"

"Nothing." She pouted.

"What is it, darling?"

Ellora bit her lip. "Do I look fat?"

Sara blinked, her cheeks flushing. "What makes you say that? Did someone say something to you?"

"No." She pulled her salwar down harder and scratched her hair.

Sara stood then, walked to her six-year-old daughter, picked her up, and sat on the bed with her. "What happened, darling? Who said what to you? Remember, no secrets from mama."

"You say it all the time, and you aren't even fat. So, what if I am fat. Must be bad to be fat, na?"

Sara's face flushed, "But moms always worry about such silly things, dear. It's complicated. I put on so much after having... Ummm... a few years ago. Then I had to work hard on losing all the weight. So...

"But kids don't have to worry about such things."

"What if I get fat and don't realize it? Maybe I should start dieting now."

"*Arre*! You don't need to do anything. You are perfect."

Ellora put her arm around her mother, "You are perfect too, Mama. The prettiest mama in all the lands."

Sara laughed, kissed her daughter, and looked at their reflection in the mirror.

love

When I first saw him, mean as it may sound, he was just " a guy" whom I was going to marry.

We'd chatted and talked, and contrary to this day and age, we both had based our choices mainly on our parents' views. We both seemed to gel on quite a few levels, and honestly speaking, I was beginning to quite like the fellow.

Besides this, he had a nice home and an even nicer family. The decision was purely practical. I'd resigned myself to the fact that love would come after marriage or even the possibility that it might never come. But of course, at quite other levels, the simple doubt was, "Would it work?" People can be very different from what they seem or, rather, the words they use.

After being burned in love, I just didn't have it in me to go through that heart-wrenching pain anymore.

So, here I was, with butterflies in my stomach, not quite encouraged by questions from thunderstruck people like, "Aren't you nervous?" or " You're getting engaged to a guy you have only spoken to online?" or "Are you sure you want to do this?

And then he was on his way back to California, probably hoping to find the same person he's had been talking to for months.

The first time I saw him at the airport, my mind went blank. I was thinking, *is this for real? Here is the person I'm about to commit my whole life to, and I'm not even sure if I know him. What about love? What about the magic of marriage?*

His eyes flitted across me with a simple hi, moving on to talk to his parents and mine. It was surreal. This guy that I had only written emails to, spoken to on the phone, was now physically present here. To get engaged to me, a girl who maybe was too broken.

I forged ahead, hoping for a sign that this too was meant to be.

We went home. His family was staying with me. For the first few days, it was difficult even to relate to the three versions of this person I had in mind. The person I wrote to, the person I spoke to, and the person in front of me, and I guess neither could he.

He hardly spoke to me at all. It was weird. He wouldn't even look at me. Was that a respectful thing or a shy thing? Did he realize that I wasn't the girl of his dreams? Maybe I didn't match his expectations and was regretting saying yes.

One day, we were finally left alone as everyone headed off sightseeing ahead of us, and we were left with the last car. As he smiled and opened the door for me, I couldn't stand it anymore,

"Do you not want to get married or something?"

"What?"

"You've hardly said three sentences to me since you came. If you don't want to get married to me, it's okay. I don't want to either. Have the guts to say so, na!"

He smiled, put his hand on my back, and guided me into the car. "It's nothing like that! It's just there are always people around us, looking. "

I waited for him to come into the car beside me. "So what if they look at us? They are family. Why can't you be yourself around them? I am around them too. "

"Maybe it's just me then. I am not as easygoing as you." He reached for my hand. "Let's start over. Hi," he says with a lopsided smile.

And there, I did find him. The few talks we had after helped me put the small pieces of the puzzle together slowly but surely. I realized the essence of the friend I'd hoped to find, and before I knew it, we were opening up doors of each other's lives and giving willful entry for free passage.

The D-day came, and though horrendously nervous, I was quite excited at the prospect of spending my life with the "friend" I was finding. After the engagement, things changed drastically, and the equation between us changed too, almost magically.

Maybe it's the effect of the ring, the one object that lets you feel almost immediately, the hold you have on another's life. We started talking the nights away with seemingly trivial matters, growing closer each minute. And how, when together, it felt like we'd known each other forever. The comfort we found with each other was like a warm blanket in the dead of winter.

I think it was more to do with the fact that when I was with him, I felt secure. As he put it once, a person has desires to be stable in two fields of life, financially and personally (referring to relationships). Materialistically, yes, I had all I could desire at the time, but personally, I was quite unstable. I had an emptiness within me, which before him, I could feel every minute and had lost all hope of filling either.

I had never met anyone remotely like him. Being with him, I could feel that I was in safe hands and that what I thought and felt mattered to someone. I must say, even though completely new to the idea of being in a relationship, he was quite willing and open to exploring every new facet with equal understanding and enthusiasm.

He always had a new perspective on things. It was like seeing a new dimension to life that I had missed seeing completely. Day by day, he seemed to become the kind of person that I'd hoped to get married to in my dreams.

Every stolen moment, every gesture, every thought or smile shared, every feeling opened a floodgate of emotions, which even I couldn't comprehend. I started feeling lucky to have him and was thankful for the gift of Him in my life.

Then a few days later, in the morning, he sat down next to me. "I leave in a few days. I just wanted to... umm..."

"Hmmm?" I smiled, teasing but wondering what he had in mind.

"I just want to make sure you are sure about

us. That you don't have any doubt about marrying me. Don't ever feel the pressure, okay? Let me know if something goes wrong or feels wrong."

I felt completely loved.

What touched me the most was, no one had shown that kind of consideration to my feelings before, ever. Someone had once told me that love begins with care.

Later that same wonderful day, standing in front of him at a mall, it hit me like a ton of bricks. This was the man I wanted to spend the rest of my life with. I was in love.

Any doubts I had were washed away like something written on sand. I started missing him, even without him ever having left me. And I think he saw it in my eyes, as I felt him realize that at that moment, no one could have loved him more.

The next few days passed in fear of his departure.

Fifteen days. That's all it took. My life had taken a turn in a new direction, and now I wasn't alone.

Before he came, I was nervous that he was coming, and by the time he left, I had tears in my eyes with the thought of him going, for I didn't want to lose this new feeling so fast. After he left, once again, we went back to chats and mails and messages and calls, but now everything seemed different and beautiful. The desire to be together, like a volcano waiting to erupt, and heaven forbid if I can make it to the day we meet again.

Till then, I know I shall be on tenterhooks, gloriously basking in the love that I share with him, cherishing each moment and rejoicing the many more to come.

For never in my dreams had I expected the person walking out the doors of the airport to transform from "a guy" to "the guy" in my life, my partner in crime, the person I always wanted by my side.

rebirth

He ran toward the lights. She was half running, half stumbling behind him, trying hard to compose herself by not laughing too hard.

"Sweetie, Abhi, hold on! I'm way too old to be running with you."

"No, you're not, Mama. You catch me all the time when we play hide and seek. Come soon."

He giggled, turning, grabbing her hand, and dragging her through the brightly decorated entrance in his puny hands.

As they walked into the fair, the pair stared, awestruck at the lights and the many rides, big and small, arranged in the park. The spicy aroma of delicious food and sweets grabbed at their nostrils, luring them deeper in.

They slowly worked their way through most of the stalls, playing games, eating too much cotton candy, sweets, and spicy fast foods, trying as many rides as they could together, all the while laughing and giggling.

Parvati marveled at the memories they were making. Just her, her son, and their life together.

As her son ran and climbed onto the carousel, she thought back to the years that lay behind these cherished moments of happiness. All the years of abuse—physical and mental. The pain, the suffering by the hands of the man who had promised to protect her, around a fire of trust.

When she had birthed as his wife, tied to him for eternity. At first, she hung onto the false hope that one day the love they had shared in their adolescence would return.

Each time he said sorry, she forgave him lovingly, praying that God graced him with a magical change. But that was not to be. His core was corrupt. Too dark for any light to get through. He, too, was brought up in a male-dominated society, spurned by a low threshold for anger. She wasn't stupid. In time, she realized it was she who had to change, but she just couldn't. Not until she had some skills to rely on for bread and butter, for she had nowhere to turn. With no parents and no support system, she was literally alone. She took classes secretly online while she had Abhimanyu, her only light and the biggest chain tying her to a miserable life. She knew he would never let her walk away with his son. So she stayed. No excuses left. Until the day he broke all barriers and did the one thing she would never forgive him for.

The monster threw their son, her heart, across the room before lunging for her. That was the day everything within her broke—giving way to the tides of anger she held within her. She beat him with the toy golf holder, and as he was down in shock and surprise, she kept hitting him till he was a mere inch of life. Warning him to stay away from them, she walked away with her son and a bag she packed every week in the hope that she would find the courage one day. To a new city, an unknown name, to never return.

"Ma, look how big he is." As she looked at the huge, beautifully decorated effigy of Ravana made every year for Dussehra at their local temple, full of fireworks. She wondered at the parallels to her life. Here stood another who once was good but got so full of his own power that he had to be stopped. As they lit the Ravana, the facsimile burst alive with flames.

As her son clapped his hands in glee, marveling at the spectacular fireworks that were now erupting, she smiled to herself. Feeling similarly purified, knowing that all evil in her life too had turned to ashes, giving way to hope and beautiful memories. A brand new start, a brand new life.

magic

“Is Santa real?”

“Why do you ask?” Bharati rustles her son’s air as they snuggle at bedtime.

“All my friends tease me about it. A lot now that Christmas is so close. They say a ten-year-old shouldn’t believe in Santa. Slater is Christian, and Moin is Muslim, and they don’t believe. They say no one has ever seen Santa.”

Bharati smiles. "Well, people choose to believe in what they choose to believe. That is where respect for all comes from. There are a lot of things people believe in, have faith in, that they haven't seen."

A pause.

"Do you think I am weird?"

Bharati raises herself up to look at her son's face, "For believing in Santa? No. I am thirty-six, and I believe in Santa. I believe in the magic that he represents. The joy of giving thoughtful presents and the warmth of the Christmas light, the beauty of the bells that jingle at different times of the day."

Anish reaches for her hands, holds them tight, and smiles. "I like that about Christmas too. Santa just brings us a couple of small presents, but it always surprises me that he knows exactly what I would like." His smile falls. "My friends say though it's parents who give the presents."

"So? You know all those Santas in the malls and in the stores that you see, all of whom are so kind and generous with their time. Them, parents, we are all simply messengers of God, Santa, whatever magic there is."

"So, is it you?"

"What?"

"Mom! Are you Santa?"

"What do you think?"

"I am not sure."

"Well, we can leave it to that for now. Though, remember, the day you stop believing in Santa is the day you become a messenger of Santa. So you either receive the magic or give the magic." Bharati pokes Anish's stomach with her finger playfully. He laughs.

"That's a nice way to look at it."

Bharati put her arm around her son and pulled him closer.

"Mom, I know why you celebrate Christmas even though we are Hindu. You always talk about how you grew up celebrating Christmas with your Christian neighbors and all that they used to do. How it reminds you of your childhood. Why does dad? Why does he choose to celebrate Christmas with us?"

Bharati grins. "Because he loves to see the joy on yours, mine and your brothers' faces while we put up the Christmas tree, decorate the house, when our elf Rudy visits, when you write your lovely letters to Santa, your excitement on Christmas morning, all our little holiday traditions.

"Besides, Dad and I believe in one God. So, if tomorrow I get a menorah and start lighting the candles for Hanukkah respectfully also, he would still be willing to celebrate with us and enjoy the warmth of the festive season. He's sweet like that."

Anish puts his arm over his mom's waist. "I like that about our family. We celebrate Diwali with all the Hindu traditions and Christmas with all our unique home traditions."

"Me too. What is important, though, is to understand the significance of any festival, for example, the spirit of Christmas, and not just enjoy the fun of traditions, decor, and gifts. None of this matters if we don't learn more about life while we do it all."

Anish nods solemnly.

"Can you tell me the story of Isaiah again? Of how he predicted the birth of Christ? I love that one."

Bharati knew there were going to be a lot of stories before Anish finally went to bed, but she loved their bedtime ritual.

dignity

She lay there on the bed. Not moving a muscle.

Her eyes watered. “It’s just the reaction to the medication,” the doctor says to her son.

No, please, no.

She blinks her eyes yes or no, but she can’t talk. She blinks her eyes yes or no, but she just lies there all day and night trying to get someone to understand; she doesn't want to live like this anymore.

She'd heard the doctor say there was a slim chance of recovery. But this pain and humiliation were not worth it.

The bills were getting higher by the hour, and her children had exhausted their bank balances and resources. They couldn't afford her lying on this bed week after week, with that slim chance.

She just wanted out!

The right to free speech. The right to bear arms. The right to choose religion.

But where is the right to choose your own end, with your dignity intact?

She regretted not creating a living will every single day! She'd had her princess beginnin gand happy ending. A memorable childhood. A doting husband. Children who made her proud in different ways.

She was satisfied with the cards life had dealt her until the day she got hit by that drunk driver.

She had no desires anymore, no complaints even. Not even with that driver, God rest his soul! She just wanted out.

Maybe, just maybe, someone would understand. She willed her fingers to move with all her might. She blinked harder. Please, just let me go!

Vengeance

She sat on the step, looking out at nothingness around her. Her eyes had concentrated onto a point above the fence. Those times when you look at empty space while your mind is actually switched off.

Her ears took in the sounds around her. A giggle here, a gurgle of laughter there. The voices of children, shouts, screams, teasing.

The world seemed to be mocking her. It refused to stop revolving just because hers was crumbling.

The sounds around pushed her further into the abyss. The abyss was full of questions she didn't want answers to.

How did she never see? Where had she lacked? Had she been so trusting or so stupid as to not see? All those words, excuses, really. All those moments when she nodded her head in understanding were actually snapshots frozen in time, proof of her blindness. Would she ever have figured it out had her phone not broken down? Would she ever have seen the truth if she hadn't come rushing three days earlier to surprise him?

A ball came thumping and hit her on her knee. She looked up, her stare harsh. "Sorry, ma'am," said a scared kid. She regained composure and picked up the ball. She passed it to him with a smile. The irony of the moment amused her. A kid. fearful of her because of his rogue ball, whereas the person who she had promised her life to had fearlessly lied to her for weeks, maybe years.

She took a deep breath.

Lifting her dead feet, one by one, she willed them to climb the stairs. The door knob felt cold to the touch as she turned it to open the door.

They didn't know she was inside the house yet. This was supposed to be their home away from home. A get away from the rigors of everyday life. She would never even have known where he was if not for a slip of the tongue.

He had to pay.

She would not go quietly like those women who worried about *what would happen to them if they broke up their marriage or if their husband left them.*

When making the vows of marriage, they had promised each other for better or worse. Maybe it actually means that they can take the liberty of being their worst with each other. Is that why people show their partners their worst sides and expect acceptance?

If this is his worst, she surely has the liberty to show her worst side. What is she willing to go through to punish him?

She stands in the hallway for a moment. The

sounds wafting to her are those of passion. They feel like embers of a fire, scorching her very soul. The memories of their happy life burned away into oblivion.

They had dreamed the American dream together. She left her family in India, her job for the kids, her business of creating one-of-a-kind decor for the home because he needed her to be with him on his trips, or so he said.

People always blame the other woman. But a marriage is a promise between two people. Another person comes between them only when they are allowed to. It is no one else's fault but his. When he, who she gave so much to, doesn't care about her or her feelings, why would a stranger? Who doesn't know her at all?!

No. It's not the "other person". She wondered if it was true love. She would have not felt bad if he had told her that he had begun to love someone else, honestly. She was sure, though, this was just a case of having your cake and eating it too.

Her feet had taken her to the kitchen.

That was where she would find her instrument

of vengeance. She took care to avoid the creaking floor boards. She tiptoed to the drawer, opened it slowly. Not a sound. She slid it out of the drawer.

She held it in her hand and moved further down the corridor, quietly. The door was ajar. They were too preoccupied to notice her standing there. The vision burned itself onto her soul. Seconds ticked away, feeling like hours. The sounds brought bile to her throat. Panting, moaning. Tears spilled out. Seconds turned to a minute, maybe two.

With resolve, she turned and walked to the main door putting her weapon into her purse.

When she was out of the house, she used all her might to slam the door shut behind her.

A few people on the street turned to look at her. She walked to her car, got in, and opened the window. Staring at the door. Waiting for him to come out.

A minute. Two. Three. It takes people a lot of time to scramble on their clothes.

When the door finally flew open, and he saw

her, his mouth fell open. His eyes went wide. His mouth made words that she was sure even he couldn't figure out.

Her smirk baffled him.

As he hurried to her, she started the car and turned the driveaway into the road. She wondered how many hits a YouTube video of a candidate running for a local office would get before the news networks got wind of it.

Yes, he would pay. In every way she could make him.

Innocence

I wonder what makes her little brain tick. The train's whooshing sound drowns out when she smiles while wiping her chocolate face with a stained handkerchief.

Her smile reminds me of the time when I was tiny too. The smile is of an innocently mischievous child.

Looking on in wonder at everyone around,

trying to imagine how they sound. With love in her eyes and questions on her lips, she dazzles everyone with her funny antics.

Another father and son cross between us, and the boy makes a face at her. She responds by sticking her tongue out and laughing. She then squeals with delight, nodding her pretty little head tight.

When another leaves, she waves goodbye and then looks back out at the pretty blue sky.

The sun shines brighter as it hits her sweet face. She's touched so many lives as she sparkles with joy unbridled.

I hope someday, a child will touch her heart and soul the same way she has touched mine. Reminding me of my days gone by and the days when I held within me the divine.

Embarrassment

All eyes were on her through those glass doors. She knew it.

Her face burned, and she wished the earth would swallow her. She stared at the disgusting food stain on his shirt, thinking of all the things she'd like to do to him right now.

Her nails bit into her fist as she tightened them. Dismissed, turning around on her heel, she walked out of the door.

People instantly looked busy, but she knew some of them had even enjoyed the scene. Others must be tutting, grabbing the phone to talk to their besties about what happened. As she walked down the corridor, she could feel carnal rage welling up from her chest through her throat until she could taste the hatred she felt. Her heart pumped so hard, she could explode.

She pushed at the glass door and rushed out into the street. She bent over and breathed hard. Taking big gulps of air, tears threatening, but she knew strangers outside wouldn't care. She looked right and left at the cars whooshing by, turned left, and kept walking. Her steps kept getting faster and faster till she found herself jogging down the pavement to nowhere.

After what felt like an eternity, "Sabah! Sabah, Wait up!" She stopped and turned around.

"What is it?" she asked tightly.

Aqueel stood there huffing and puffing. Man, he needed exercise. How should he handle this? One wrong turn, and this would blow up in his face. He'd just had lunch, and his stomach was hurting from the sprint he had to take to catch up with her. But he'd heard, and he knew he had to go see if she was okay.

"What is it?" A bit louder this time.

"Uh..." He took a deep breath, taking a step closer. "I just wanted to see if you were okay."

"Okay? Okay?" Even louder. "Define okay."

He raised his hands and shrugged his shoulders helplessly. "Hey! I just meant if you need to talk or something."

She looked miserable. Eyes raging, watering, almost to tears. He felt bad for her. "What the hell was that about? He's a jerk. Everyone knows that. Everyone talks about it. So what if he was a jerk one more time to you in a totally new way?"

"I cannot believe the things he said to me. I just wanna go home and hug my kids!"

He touched her elbow and steered her toward the coffee shop. "Let's just go have a cup of coffee."

He sat her down at a corner table and ordered two cappuccinos. He could see the fire in her eyes as she muttered, "I don't want coffee. I would rather have his head on a platter."

"That won't make you feel as good as your favorite coffee, trust me. And then we'll think about food." he encouraged.

"I wasn't being funny! And you are not winning any competition either." She jerked with realization. "You heard! That means by now, everyone at work knows. Shit! What an effective grapevine we have. Oh my God." She pulled at her hijab. "I'm so mortified."

"It's okay, you know? Like you said, he's a jerk. It's not a big deal! Why are you letting it affect you so much?"

"You weren't there; you didn't hear the things he said to me. It wasn't that bad an idea. The result wasn't a total disaster either. I don't know what the hell his problem is. It was as if he was venting out all his life frustrations on me. So rude... so loud... so sinister! He said that I was thinking all wrong, wondering if I had a brain even. That I shouldn't even have put those designs forward without consulting with him. That I insulted his intelligence and the company blah blah blah! He made me sound so stupid... I don't want to remember. Maybe I am an idiot. I hate this job."

"That's bullshit, and you know it! Everyone, and I mean everyone, knows you are talented and have brilliant ideas. You love what you do, and it shows. He's your boss. He's not your friend. He doesn't have to be nice. If he is, that's a bonus for us. And it's not like he's not thrown a backhanded compliment your way now and then. Hell! You're like the star employee."

"Yeah, right!" she mumbled.

"You know I'm right." He grinned at her, pushing the coffee toward her. "Maybe that's why it's hurting so much, because it's the first time. You need to get over this. It's not as big a deal as you're making it."

She raised her eyes to look at him questioningly.

He continued softly, "Hey, I'm not taking sides. Sure, he's surpassed himself. He had no right to behave that way. What happened was way out of line. But you've been working here for what? Two years now? He's been coming up the ladder for years. Everyone knows how he is, but he gets the job done. You went over his head, and he couldn't take it. Lucky for him, you slipped finally.

"You have yet a long way to go, here and in life. If you let things like this get to you, no one but you gets affected. Unless you're thinking of resigning on one horrid day, but that way, you won't get anywhere. This is an office, babe; it's bound to be hard, people will be manipulative, confusing... that's the game. But it's where your salary comes from. Very few people get a job that they enjoy doing. You're taking this hard cos' for the first time; your aptitude, talent has been questioned. But that doesn't mean you're useless. That just means what you did today was not just not right for the project at hand."

She deflated in front of him. Her eyes glistened up, and a tear rolled down as she let go of all the pent-up rage. She wiped it with one hand.

"Yeah, but how will I face him again, all those people?" She looked at him, sniffling like a lost puppy.

He squeezed her hand and smiled. "Hey! Only those who haven't been under the firing squad can be on the squad, right? Besides, why do you even care? There's a quote on this, right? I think something about people who are your friends not caring and those who are bitchy are definitely not friend material. Maybe this will help you differentiate."

A twinkle crept to her eyes. "The silver lining."

He beamed. "Yup. The silver lining."

"You are a good friend. Let's sit here a while longer." With that, she picked up the coffee, had a long sip, and looked out the window.

"As long as you need. Then let's get back to doing what we do, our best every day."

Soulmate

"Arre! At least try it once."

"Why, Ma?" Nimisha whined. She snuggled deeper into her blanket and looked out at the city from their balcony. She usually loves these late evening chats with her mom... until today.

"Is there another boy?"

"No."

"Girl?"

"No!"

"Then what is the problem?"

"What about love?"

"All that comes with time, dear."

"Passion?"

"What kind of nonsense is that?! That you would know only after marriage, na. Plus, that too comes usually." Her mom's words trailing off in the end didn't provide any encouragement.

"There is no possible way anyone can guarantee that."

"Who says marry the first person you meet? This is dating, as you youngsters say, with family's permission. Talk to him, meet him. Don't like him. We will find someone else."

"It's that easy?!"

"It's that easy." Here, mom smiled, sipping her chai.

"What if I meet a guy, like him, fine, and then there's someone else out there? Someone meant for me. And then I meet him after I get married to the guy who was just fine?" She rolled her eyes.

"*Aga, sacchii.* Destiny is something magnificent. That spark happens only with a few. Soul mates are overrated. You want a companion, a comfortable life, and someone you can be yourself with."

"Are you yourself with baba?

"Baba and I are solid. I love him because I love you. Our love is within you. Through you. "

"Haven't you ever loved anyone?"

Aai's eyes moved away, finding the moon to settle on.

"Once."

"You never told me before?"

"No one asked me before. Plus, it's not nice to talk about these things." Aai rubbed her finger on her cup of chai.

"Why, Aai? It was a part of your life. Are you ashamed?"

Aai's eyes jerked to daughter, now old enough tounderstand,maybe.

"No. Just full of regret. And questions."

"What happened?" Nimisha insisted.

"A lot of passion, as you say, but no guts to fight with my parents for him."

Nimisha's next question was a whisper. "Did you love him?"

"Deeply," Aai said quietly.

"Was he the love of your life?"

She paused, looked at her cup, looked up, grinned, and winked. "One of them!"

"Aai! Kuch bhi. Were you kidding this whole time?" Nimisha slapped her mom's knee and laughed.

"You will never know. After all, a lot of boys loved my long hair and gajra." Aai smiled. Nimi sha grinned. Holding her coffee, knowing there must be some truth to it.

"Coming back to you. What do you think?"

"But I won't *know* him know him. These people you want me to meet." NImisha sighed.

"Get to know them. Whose telling you to get married to the first donkey that comes your way?" Nimisha's eyes popped. "Don't look at me like that. They are all the same if you ask me. But your generation likes to try out things. So try them out, like a piece of jewelry in the mirror. See how they look on you. How you look with them. How you feel with them. If you like it, buy it."

"Aaiiiii!" Nimisha threw her hands up in the air.

"What! That's what your dating is, na? You all date, meet people, try it out for a while, maybe move in together but one day decide that you don't like each other. And take a while to heal and all that sad songs business. In an arranged marriage, you at least have the getting to know you magical phase that lasts a few years before you go into the "I'm bored of you phase," by which time you have kids, and life is exciting again... That's just how it is... Anyway, it's up to you what you want to do.

"All I ask of you is, he should be from a decent family, well educated with a good, stable job so that we don't have to worry about you after marriage. It should be a relief, not added stress that don't know what will happen after. Someone who can afford to take you to places and have good money sense."

"Hmmm."

"You know, you could have saved me all this trouble if you had found a boy for yourself."

"Ab nahi mila toh kya kaoon!? It's not like there are great boys everywhere. Not everyone is marriage material!"

Aai snapped her fingers and pointed at her. "Exactly! Your gut knows what marriage material is. Meet these boys and find someone who you feel in your gut is marriage material and pick him."

"What if I am wrong?" Nimisha sipped her coffee, looking at the fall from her twentieth-story balcony.

"All this talk of soulmates. We don't have just one. Anyone who completes a part of our soul is our soulmate. You have to be your own soulmate first. Job, husband, kids. All this doesn't matter if you are not happy with yourself. If you are happy with yourself, then everything can become good. Don't look for happiness in another person. Don't put that pressure on a man. They are too weak for that. You have to know your soul first." Aai pointed her finger to her own chest and then moved her hand to place it on Nimisha's.

"We are your soulmates too. You can always come back home."

Nimisha smiled and sighed. "Acha Dikhao. Where are all these boys you want to show me..."

Aai slapped her hands together. "Yeh hui na baat! Wonderful!" She picked up her phone, opened WhatsApp, and started scrolling through photos.

"Your masi sent this. He is already in Florida. 75k a year. Software only. But this boy your aunt Nita sent works in Amazon. His package is lower, but in the future, he will surely go to the US, na. Prospects are good... This one gets five lakh per month but works in India only." Aai made a face. "Bonus here is, you would be close to us, and this one..."

perfection

As she held her breath under water, she smiled. “This is it!”

Tomorrow would be everything she dreamed of. Shaina came out of the bath, gasping, feeling renewed. Drying herself, she stepped into the walk-in closet and browsed through the variety of dresses, mentally trying on and discarding each one.

The parade in front of the imaginary mirror

lasted only so long before she got impatient and worried that once again, she had nothing to wear. It was then that the image of the clothes long-forgotten crept shyly into the front of her mind. She dragged the pile of dresses and dusters from the back and pulled out combinations she thought would work. Two, three tries later, she decided on a silver and black off-shoulder choli with a burgundy skirt, an Indo western duster, and brown boots. The color went well with her recently dyed hair, her brown skin, and hazel eyes.

She completed the ensemble with silver hoops and a silver purse.

She stood back and admired her work in the mirror and decided there was something to an ideal dress for the perfect occasion. Feeling confident, she stepped out of her apartment and walked down the flight of steps out the front door.

Having spent the whole morning at the spa, she was feeling totally rejuvenated. Ready to take on the world, she took a deep breath in the crisp night air and smiled at the many harrowing days of preparations that had got her to this day.

She could feel herself glowing under the moonlit night. She smiled to herself. Touch wood, she thought as she touched her head for good luck. This is what dreams are made of. Hersanyway.

As the car pulled up, she felt faint with anticipation. Her heart fluttered at the mere sight of him. He got out of the car, smiling at her admiring the vision she created.

She could see in his eyes the love he had for her. He kissed her lightly and whispered, "I can't wait to take that dress off you someday." She felt her heart would just jump out of her body, resonating with the love she had for him. She smirked at him, and as they settled into the car, her thoughts were consumed with images of what tomorrow was going to be like.

All the plans were laid out. She was a tyrant when organizing events were concerned. And after all, this was her wedding!

Super expensive, with guests from around the world, and food too. A visual treat that would fuel every sense. Dancing every night and chanting all morning. A big fat Desi wedding. With the evolving world, this was another thing that had also gotten bigger and bolder, with traditions morphing.

Roka. Mehendi. Sangeet. Wedding. Vidaai. And all of it streamed live from the resort by the seaside.

Nothing and no one would come between her and perfection. She had worked like a drill sergeant, mapping out the minutest details along with the wedding planner. No head passed by that wasn't bitten off. She was very well aware that everyone around had been walking on pins and needles on account of her yelling. But she was unabashed—It was all going to be worth it.

People would be talking about this wedding for years to come.

Tomorrow, the fruits of all her efforts would finally pay off. Vivid pictures danced in front of her eyes as she imagined what the day was going to be like, from how everyone would love her lehenga, to the walk down the aisle along with her cousins and brother, to the wedding, to how he'd be looking at her to the reception, the dancing, the fun, and the trip to Bora Bora after. She couldn't wait to Instagram her honeymoon.

Tomorrow, she would have everything.

The perfect family, the perfect job, and the man of her dreams to share the rest of her life with.

She was amazed at how time flew. It seemed like it was two years ago that she had been introduced to Jayant. And before she knew it, she was head over heels in love. Well, it was something like love, she was sure of it. Their families had introduced them, and her mom had said, "Such a wealthy family. They will treat you like a princess and give you the life you deserve." She found every aspect of him and his life fascinating. Rich and successful, living the life of movie stars.

Since childhood, she had known she deserved to live among the rich. Sure, she had worked hard to get where she was as well, but thank goodness she had never gone through the melodrama she had seen other girls go through. That had put her off boys and men at an early age. Early on, she had decided that she would wait for the perfect man to cross her path. Someone who ticked off all her boxes and pursued her earnestly before she committed to him for the rest of her life.

She had always known she was beautiful

enough, someone most brown parents would want for their son. Fair, big eyes, long hair, tall, cultured, an amazing dancer, and working no less. She was a catch and from a family that was vegetarian to boot.

That is why even when Jayant had come into her life, she had avoided saying the magic words before she was absolutely sure of his devotion toward her. "You are gorgeous," were his first words to him. He pursued her relentlessly. Texts. Flowers. Presents. Fancy restaurants. And long drives in his Porsche. She remembered when he had said, "Mom has decided you have to be her bahu, and she always gets her way!"

She giggled inwardly, glancing across at the man who now held her future in his hands. The ring she'd picked out for herself before their engagement sparkled on her finger.

They both were on the highway leading to the restaurant, where finally, they were getting some time off from all the family and friends and wedding planning.

"It is considered bad luck, yeh ladka ladki meeting before the wedding," Nani had fumed, but grandparents say that stuff all the time.

Jayant had insisted she have a 'me' day before the big day. And who says no to the jawaii of the house?!

The excited conversation around their itinerary in Bora Bora was interrupted with two rings from his mobile. She was surprised to notice that for the first time in a year, the phone was lying in the space between the seats. Usually, he was quite fierce about his privacy. His phone was quite off bounds.

She looked at him quizzically, reaching for the phone. "Want me to see who it is?"

"Must be someone from the caterers. I'll get it later," he said, waving her off.

"You know, since we are getting married now, I think it's time that I get phone privileges." She smirked.

"What do you mean?" He looked at her warily.

She giggled. "Well, I am almost your wife now, and there's no point in you being so possessive about your phone now. The only thing you should be possessive about is me. I can help take care of things. After all, if you're so busy with other things, who'll take care of me?" She suggestively slid her hand up this thigh. "

"We'll have to see about that, won't we? I can't wait for tomorrow, my love." He grinned, taking her hand and kissing it softly.

She was feeling deliciously naughty. They had waited and waited, and she was excited to see what all the hoop-la around sex was. When the phone rang again, she snapped the phone up. Before he could say anything, she had answered the call. Before he could protest, she tapped on the speaker, laughing. "Hello?"

"What the fuck? Where the hell have you been? I told you not to hang up on me when I'm talking to you!" The raspy, really angry female voice snapped.

"You don't need to take that tone with me. I'm on my way out. I said I'll call you back, and I will. Give me fifteen minutes to get back to you. Bye," he said officially, still sounding edgy. He reached for the phone, but Shaina was reaching to do the same, and the person continued, "I don't care what you are doing. You've been giving me the go-around for days now. If I hadn't been calling from different numbers, you wouldn't even be picking up my calls. I'm not going to—"

"That's enough. I'll talk to you when you've cooled down. You need to put down the phone now!"

Shania looked at Jayant, wondering what this was about. He smiled at her reassuringly, but his eyes belied his lips. He was clearly tense. He stretched his hand to snatch the phone, and she moved it out of reach.

"Are you with someone? You better not be with that bitch. You told me you were on your way home. You promised me that you'd stay away from her and break off the wedding. I know I'm not as ideal as a little miss perfect, whose filthy rich daddy is going to pull you out of your self-dug grave of debt. Trust me, if I didn't absolutely have to, I would never have gotten into a mess like this with a loser like you. But here I am. and here you are. You better own up to this baby, or I'm going to bring your sorry ass down with me."

The last few words were garbled as Shaina dropped the phone in shock. He wrestled to get to the phone from the floor, looking at her frantically, saying, "She's crazy. I don't know what she's talking about. She's got me confused with someone else. Baby..."

Her hand flew to her mouth as shock gripped her heart.

"What's happening there? I'm not going to take any more shit from you. I don't care who's listening to me because I'm about ready to start shouting off rooftops. You promised me money, which also you skipped on, and I'm stuck five months pregnant, and now it's too late for me to get rid of it too. I could *kill* you. My figure is ruined forever! Do you hear me?"

As the caller screamed her lungs out, Shania started screaming for him to stop the car. Jayant tried getting to the phone and physically held her hands to avoid her getting out of the car.

Before they knew it, the headlights up front were right in their faces. He tried swerving around it with panicked eyes, but the car revolted against his reflexes, and the car went into a tailspin and went plummeting down the hill.

Her last thought before her world went blank was *nothing* is ever perfect.

compassion

Avina looked up as she heard the shouting. She kept the plate she was about to load into the dishwasher aside and looked out the window.

A smile crept to her lips as she saw her children running around their uncle Keshav.

They giggled and pushed each other out of the way so as not to run into him.

He was exhausted from playing blind man's bluff with them, and now, his eyes followed them around, pleased with their gaiety. He shielded his eyes against the sun. He looked at his pocket, gently unfolding his towelette to wipe his hands and face. He put it back in his pocket and then patted it to check if he had done it. She sighed.

It had been a long journey, and at times, when she stopped to think, she felt overwhelmed even now. Other days, like this one, made her feel that every excruciating, perilous moment was worth it. After all, they had come a long way, so it was important to appreciate the journey, right?

The past flashed before her eyes like snapshots taken in haste.

Running toward the car as her mom and dad came home with her baby brother.

Shrieking with joy when Kiki threw a ball back to her the first time.

Making use of the bed like a trampoline, taking turns jumping, and trying to go higher and higher.

Studying together, with mom scolding them to

write and spell properly.

Lying in bed, telling him stories, playing silly games with words or make-believe characters.

Coming home with her medal for painting for the first time, hugging her baby brother before rushing to her parents.

Her parents hooting from the stands, encouraging Kiki to take that six. She even now remembered thinking how her dad had come for her brother's cricket match but never her running. She had wondered if her parents clapped any harder, their palms would probably catch fire. Her dad pushed through her and a sea of kids to get at his son, who won man of the match!

Dad pushed Kiki to practice harder, punishing him with his belt if he said no to practicing.

The constant abuse as the man they loved so much drowned himself in a passion of winning by proxy.

Being told to shut up when she tried to come between them.

Being rebuked for her medals, because what

future does a woman in sports have?

That day in the garden, when she went looking for him, the horror she felt as she saw Kiki skipping. Running to him, seeing the tears in his eyes, telling him to stop, and being shocked by his response that he just couldn't.

Mom held him close after he fell down in exhaustion after working out for three hours without water.

Even at that young age, she knew it was not normal. Dad smiled at his son's enthusiasm as she shivered in fear of what was happening to both of them. Dad slapped her for taking her mom's side that maybe Kiki needed to slow down, and he, their father, needed to just stop.

Rushing into the bathroom when Kiki didn't come down for dinner, to see him washing his hands. She could still feel the taste of her own tears as she applied lotion to his hands, burned from the boiling water. He'd said, "But Didi, my hands aren't clean yet."

The small habits that slowly and surely developed grew into necessities. Checking if all the doors were locked three times. Washing his hands, feet, and face five times before eating or sleeping, or going out even.

Running for exactly thirty-eight minutes before eating his lunch.
Eating only boiled vegetables.
Wiping anything with disinfectant before touching it.
Counting steps as he walked.
Not liking others touching him.
Having everything that belonged to him in a perfect way and retaliating if anything ever was kept awry.

The doctor sternly tells her parents that they should have come to him months ago.

Holding her brother's hands gingerly as he took his medications each night.

Soothing him with her voice as he cried to sleep. Getting frustrated as his brother kept slipping into the same habits again and again.

Going off to college, hoping her brother got better magically while she was away. The denial felt like a relief.

Coming back to realize it had been such a

mistake to have left him with a weak mother and uncaring father. Each time she came back, she noticed that he got quieter, more reserved. His "quirks" increased. Leaving to go back to the hostel early to get away from the darkness.

She was having so much fun being by herself, doing her own thing, enjoying the freedom from that restricting household that she chose not to see what was happening. She thought she deserved that much happiness. That was probably the worst thing she could have done.

On a rare visit, she learned that even the home schooling had been stopped. She'd opened the door to his room to see a broken boy, now fifteen, sitting in a corner. It was like the desire to live was squeezed out of him. She'd tried talking to him, but he seemed not to hear.

She recollected the ensuing screaming match she had with her parents. They thought he was better off cut off from the world. He couldn't function normally anyway. Why torture him?

They couldn't bear the stares they got from people, they said. Her father spat every word of hatred, talking about the possibilities he had and what he had become. The man she called spouted venom. Who was she to talk to? She was far away from it all. She didn't have to see him like they had. They had to take care of him every day, and they weren't getting younger. And on and on it went.

Finally, she'd packed her things and Kiki's and left with him.

It had been hard, the progress slow, but just by trying to keep things normal, there had been a kind of normalcy introduced into their lives. She guided him, took him for his doctor's visits regularly, and talked to him. The medications helped. She stayed by him 24/7. Luckily, she could get a job working from home.

She told him each and every time he reached for the door with a napkin or checked the appliances that everything was fine. Slowly, he began to trust her way of doing things.

She went to the park with him, took long walks, took him to the market, ignoring the skeptical looks they got. He responded by taking baby steps.

Steps that, though tiny to the naked eye, were humongous leaps of faith for him, and she knew enough to appreciate it. Her parents came to visit, bearing gifts and financial support, and even changed their attitude for the better after seeing the steady growth in Kiki's character.

She remembered the day her father cried for forgiveness as to what he had done, the horrors finally catching up to him. She had told him to do better now that he knew better.

Kiki was slowly growing into a young man, displaying the sparks of originality that made him who he was. He'd even taken to drawing and cooking, and they had their bit of fun doing things they enjoyed together. His smiles warmed her heart. It was the nectar she needed for her own soul. Through all this, she met the sweetest man ever who understood her responsibilities and shared them happily with her equally, if not more. Eventually, they married and were blessed with two tiny angels. The two angels, who were now playing tic-tack-toe with their uncle watching. His gaze spoke volumes about how much love he had within.

"What are you doing, darling?" Her husband came behind her, putting his arms around her.

"Oh, just looking at the loves of my life." She

enveloped his arms with her own.

“Hmmm. Quite a sight they make. Sandra has come asking for Keshav. She’s sitting outside.”

“She’s been so good for Keshav, don’t you think? It was a stroke of luck that we joined that sushi-making class where we met her. He’s had friends before, but no one like her. They talk for hours, and she understands his needs. Not just by words, by action even. She’s so kind and loving. Have you noticed his improvement is exponential since they met?” Avina speculated.

“Yeah! I think there might even be something brewing there. It’s obvious she wants to help, and he wants to be helped. He listens to her, tries to please her. Who knows? Kiki might finally have the one thing everyone craves. “

Avina turned, looked at her husband, and looked out the window again. “I hope so. I do hope so. “Hope and love—that’s all one needs to live on, live strong...”

disgust

He stood at the door, looking at her rush to open it

He had returned home happy, finally willing to shed the fears. No more disappearing acts for him from now on, no siree! She flung open the door for him and hugged him tightly.

“You look good, Jeevan!” Her tone was proud. “Have you been working out?” she wondered, and he heard a snicker bubbled up. He hugged her back with a hand, the other hand holding the trolley bag.

"Yes, Amma. I try to keep in shape." Jeevan winked.

"That's good. Well, come on in. You look exhausted. I've made your favorites. Have to fatten you up. "

Jeevan rolled his eyes but walking into his home was still daunting.

The steps across the threshold were the hardest he had ever taken. Everything seemed new yet old, in its context with him. The furniture had been moved around but was the same. The rooms had a dusty feel about them. Looked like his mom had lost her fanatical cleaning streak. The photos were all there, a layer of dust on them. The medals, the games, the plays. He reflected on those moments with fondness.

His coat shed, he got comfortable, and soon it was like he had never left. They laughed and joked, talking about the old times as she toddled around the kitchen, making chai to accompany the samosas and halwa she had made. His mom was still the best cook in the world, and he ate like he had been hungry for ages.

After tea, he went for a shower and took her for a walk. She pointed out the streets to him with excitement, pointing out the changed store names and whose child was up to what now. He smiled at her indulgently.

The walk home was quiet, and he placed a hand on her shoulder as they walked.

"I have made your favorite dinner. Bhindi, khatti meethi daal and roti with that achar you love. I picked it just yesterday."

"I am sure it is great. *Aao baitho,*" he insisted they make the rotis together.

The banging started just before nightfall. They were still at the dining table, chatting. They looked at each other, startled. She wiped her hands on her pallu, rushed to the door, and backed away from the screen in revulsion.

"*KHOL!* What are you looking at! Open it fast." His father's shouts were garbled. His mother stood firm.

"Nahi. I told you not to come back till you change

your mind. And in this state, I doubt your mind is working even."

Silence. Then softly, "I heard."

Her head tilted sideways toward her son with sadness, and she nodded. Jeevan stood up and went to the door, the thin screen dividing the two, protecting whom?

The moonlight shone over them like a spotlight.

"Ah! Aa gaya. The prodigal son has returned." The disdain in his father's voice made him wince as he saw the hand he waved at him and remembered the last beating.

And then, with a burst of energy, before anyone could react, his father's foot was smashed through the door, and he was in.

"No one stops me from entering my own home. Especially. Not. You." His finger pointed at Amma's chest. The spittle flew everywhere as he shot every word with rage.

Jeevan came forward, standing between them.

“Appa!” he said, his voice meek with fear.

His father guffawed, and then his voice went deathly quiet.”Don’t you call me father, you sick son of a bitch! You think you can come between us? Well, think again, big man.” Appa smirked.

He cut to the side, toward the table, and picked a knife unsteadily. He addressed his wife, brandishing the knife.

“How dare you? How dare you let him into our home? This piece of shit who killed my daughter. My lovely, sweet, innocent darling daughter.” Tears filled his eyes. His shoulders slumped as memories flooded his being.

“I taught her how to walk. Her laughter, the way she called me, my innocent daughter. I dreamed of her wedding, and where is she now...” His voice cracked with sobs, the knife fell, and he was almost bent over, hands on his face, in surrender.

The night was silent. His mother laid a hand on Jeevan’s arm and nudged him to the side.

“With time, you will love him the same way. Jasmine is no more. You need to accept it, for our family's sake. He is all we have..." The weight of the love in those words brought Jeevan's head down.

"You!" He looked up at Jeevan. "I will never forgive you." He spat, and with the last word in the air, he grabbed the knife back and lunged at Jeevan, cutting his arm. The blood stained both of them, the blood they shared.

When he came back to slash again, Jeevan stepped and grabbed his father's hand away. They wrestled for the knife as Jeevan used all his strength to push the man he called a father out of the door.

"*Ruko. Ruko.* Stop this." Her voice went heedless. A few seconds felt like an eternity as they struggled.

"STOP!" the bellow shattered the angry haze.

They both turned to see the woman who had never raised her voice in her whole life. The same woman now held a gun in her hands, leveled at her husband.

"Get out of my house! I will not let you hurt him." The quiet steel in her voice shocked both men.

The man she had promised to never leave looked at both of them, lost as if seeing them for the first time. With listless feet, he stumbled out the door and into the night without a word.

She proceeded to bandage his arm. Terror gripped Jeevan's heart. "What if he does something stupid, Amma? I should go get him."

She had cupped his face in her hand and said, "He won't. He is too weak. He will come back in his own time. Deep down, he loves you too. And no matter what he says or does, it doesn't change the fact that you are all we have. They will all have to eventually accept it. Now help me fix this door."

When night fell, he covered her sleeping form with the blanket and went out into the hall. The photos along the mantelpiece and walls beckoned him. He touched them lightly. Jasmine with the medals. Jasmine in the plays. Jasmine rejoiced with her teammates. So full of life, yet...

Sadness engulfed him. His father was right. He had killed Jasmine. But people would have to eventually see that he had no choice.

Jasmine had never been happy. The mirror had taunted her for years before she had decided the path she wanted to take and left home as soon as she could work. She had never wanted to be a girl. It had taken years, but her transition to Jeevan was inevitable.

It was not going to be easy, but the journey had begun, and now it was just a matter of time before the world accepted that Jasmine was no more.

His mother had been the first to know his secret. That was when he had discovered, it takes a strong woman to love her child, no matter who they are inside, unconditionally.

pride

Those eyes look yonder,
Looking upward,
In total wonder...
How she came to this.
Once upon a time,
It was her, at the center of the universe,
A metronome, her body.
Beats in her feet.
Now the stars have shifted,

Times have changed anew.
And shine brighter on this star
This torchbearer of the future.
This part of her outside of her,
Her heart is in rhythm...
dancing, scared, beaming,
Eyes twinkle brightly, a smile grows...
Fabricating dreams with every movement.
Unsure, she and her. Fearful of the end.
Awkward movements off the beat,
Hesitant smiles remembering all mom said.
An vision she never imagined possible,
Seeing her little one shimmer so bright.
Surrounded by applause.
A supportive gesture that binds them all.
Nothing ever compares to this,
This joy that a mother feels.
Finding that first costume,
Prepping tirelessly for those few moments on a dais.
The joy she feels reaches a crescendo,
And pride overshadows it all!
Seeing their child under that blinding spotlight.
Created by her adoring gaze.

A memory cherished forever
As the light of her passion gets passed on...

Comparison

"Divya's son also got into the gifted program." Vani fretted as she mopped her floors shiny.

"Hmmm..." Ravi kept scrolling through his phone.

"Suman's son got in last year."

"What are you saying, Vani?" Ravi knew what she was saying, but he was tired. The day was ending, and he wanted to go to bed.

"Nothing!" She continued mopping the floor, her daily bedtime ritual.

"It's okay. Things will work out for Riya when it is meant to. There is no need to rush these things."

"But Riya is smart enough. What is it that they have that she doesn't? The teacher recommended her this year, but she still didn't get in."

Ravi waited. He knew there was more, as always.

"At her age, I was top in school, always first. I don't know what I am doing wrong with her. It is so upsetting. You don't understand. You don't sit with her at all!"

"Are you done?"

Vani went still. Then she began wringing the handle of the mop till her hands went red.

"Okay! Step away from the mop and sit down here. Next to me."

Vani sat down next to her hubby. He rubbed her back gently. She slumped down on the sofa, deflated.

"You do realize you cannot control your daughter's successes and failures, right? She is a perfectly happy, content, and smart child. No amount of trophies or programs can change that, unless... unless you start making her feel that she is less than another."

Vani's mouth flew open, her hand to her face. "I would never do that!"

Ravi smiled. "Not consciously. But when you fret about her grades, it shows. Stress is contagious. Also, when you comment about other kids doing better in some things, she obviously hears that. Hearing is her superpower, after all."

Vani's face fell. "Why am I failing her? Is there something that others know of and we do not?. Savita's son is doing sixth grade math in fourth grade. Suman's daughter won the first prize for creative writing. She is a bright girl. I must be doing something wrong."

Ravi smiled. "Maybe. Maybe not. Maybe we are the correct ones by letting her grow at her own pace. After all, life is a marathon, na. Not a sprint. There is no guarantee that someone who does well in their formative years goes on to succeed and vice versa. Look at me, I was last in class till the eighth standard in India, and then I flourished in college. You were top and then chose to keep things laid back for Riya's sake. Else you would have been VP by now too."

"I wish I had a magic eight ball to tell a future or a talisman to make her successful and happy in life!" Vani sighed.

"Since we have neither, for now, let's just do our best and take each day as it comes. I see you trying your best to stay on top of all her work, reminding her to do what needs to be done, finding her the right resources, helping her understand when she can't. There is not much else you can do... humanly, that is.

"If you find some magic amulet, then sure, please use it. But then also, remember. There is always a price to pay." He snickered, putting his hands across his chest like a Genie and winking.

Vani laughed. "You are right. I need to let these things go. Not get to me. " She took a deep breath and got up to wipe down the kitchen counter. Another nightly ritual.

Ravi smiled to himself. Stress managed... *Till the next time someone's child achieves something that our child hasn't. Poor thing. A severe case of anxiety rooted in comparisonitis.*

Shame

Why and how could life have become so twisted? As she stood there thinking about all that's gone by. The shivering, swaying leaves seemed to be calling out to her. The city lights afar seemed to be taunting her, beckoning her to let her mind wander to the deep recesses of her morbid thoughts.

It didn't seem that long ago that she had first come into the city. Alone but happy to finally be free of the constant battering of her fragile soul.

It had taken courage, but she had taken the final step out of the house that gave her nothing but pain. Gathering the last shreds of her confidence, she had taken a fresh stab at life. A new country, a new job, a new lease on life.

Only to end up in daily torment.

She still remembered his hands on her. His touch. The stench of expensive perfume. His disgusting whispers in her ear, so close, promising the world in exchange for silence. How it had taken all her strength to overcome the fears of being out on the street again.

How revolted she had felt, finally touching him to push him away. How her hand had stung after it met his cheek. The satisfying sound filled her soul with rage.

How everyone had but stared at her as she walked out crying, knowing she had to begin life anew. She knew the consequences. She knew the gossip that would go around about her now. Lies wrapped in half-truths would circle the world via tweets, texts, and snide conversations by strangers.

She will soon have gone from employee of the

year to "The girl who..."

The pain was too much to bear. She had thought she was strong and now time was once again testing how much she could take before breaking into the tiny pieces of whatever it was that held her together in the first place.

There has to be a reason why all this is happening. And the reason was maybe that she just wasn't meant to be. Maybe she was a mistake of nature that was being erased bit by bit. Every step of the way, she only got knocked down as soon as she stood up from the last fall. No more.

From the postman who touched her hand to the uncle who rubbed her shoulder. To her family that blamed her for her fiancé cheating on her. All of it was labeled as her fault.

She wouldn't take any more. She wasn't going to give life the chance to knock her off her feet again. Here, she was in control. No one else. Everything was in her hands. She had no one to call her own.

She wiped her eyes before the tears came flooding and looked over the skyline. The thought occurred that once she did this, there was no turning back. No one could stop her, and no one could bring her back. No one wanted her in the first place, but then who cared now? She was finally taking matters into her own hands. She was going to do this, and then, well, only those who've already tried it before may know...

"Miss, are you okay?" asked the man with concerned eyes.

She turned to face him, eyes blank and dead. "Yes. I am fine."

"So, are you going to do it? "

"Yes! "

She put her foot forward and climbed into the roller coaster.

Gritting her teeth, she settled into the seat, trembling as she buckled herself with the belt straps along her shoulders. As the bar came down across her thighs, panic took hold of her, and she gripped the bars in front of her so hard that her knuckles turned white. She drew a worried glance from the kid sitting next to her, but she was more worried about the wave of nausea that threatened her.

As the coaster started rattling forward, she tried to think positively and what this might mean for her, but with every rattle, she felt the second hand of the clock of doom ticking toward her. Her stomach lurched as bile came forth. It brought back memories she swallowed.

Just as they reached the top and looked down, hysteria overcame her. She looked around for someone to help her get off but seeing everyone's smiling faces, she realized that the only way was down.

As the cars started tipping downward. She held her breath and closed her eyes shut, and remembered all the times that she needed her to stand up for herself.

The coaster plunged down.

Her past flashed through her mind, bringing forth a renewed rage. The screams around her expressed all the joy and fear embroiled into the exhilaration of the moment. The person next to her seemed to be screaming his lungs out as they fell again, higher, lower, farther into the air. Then she heard him screaming words in her direction.

"Open your eyes. Feel the rush, maaaaaan! This is the lifeeeeeee!"

She opened her eyes and decided to forget that once upon a time, she had sworn to never look out of windows higher than three floors. As the coaster ascended into the sky, she felt herself turning around in more ways than one.

She started screaming, out of fear or relief no one would know. But she screamed till her throat felt sore. The blood started rushing up and down her body. More twists and turns. She felt faint. Before she knew it, her screams turned into shouts of laughter, and the butterflies floating in her stomach became a thrill. With each rotation, she felt a new breath of life being pushed into her, giving her the strength to face whatever else life throws at her.

As the earth rushed up at her once again, she could feel all her fears falling out of her like bricks from a roof. The last inversion brought forth the feeling of her life being magically transformed. And then, just as she let out a final cry of exuberant relief for all the pain she was leaving behind, the ride came to its clattering end.

She looked around and took a deep breath of elation, having conquered her biggest fear. The park host looked at her and smiled with understanding. “Are you feeling better now?”

She laughed. “Sure am. I finally got a knack for it now. I’m going to have more fun with it the next time round. Should I get back in line to go again?”

When she finally left the park, cotton candy in hand, she was ready to restart her life again! She was free from the burden of shame, which was never hers to begin with.

frustration

"My tummy gets so upset eating spicy food, na. Thanks so much for making this special for me." Shafika preened.

Aleema smiled tightly and nodded. Would have been nice for you to help, she thought. Shoaib placed a hand over her hand, stroking it with his thumb. He nodded at her, closing his eyes, encouraging her to stay calm. He spoke for her, knowing Aleema was at her limit. "It's no problem. How was your day today? Found a house yet?"

"*Arre kahan!* There are no good houses out there anymore. But don't worry. We will be out of your hair soon." She smiled at her seven-year-old son, who was dropping the daal everywhere over the dining table.

"*Beta* Nabeel. Please don't do that," Aleema said through her teeth, wondering for the nth time when Shafika would take the trouble to parent her child. Nabeel made a face and jumped off the table to go jump on the couch.

"Sayid, please take Nabeel's plate to the kitchen."

Sayid, now ten, rolled his eyes and did the needful. Shafika laughed. "Kids these days! Can't do anything about them."

Aleema gripped her spoon and said to herself, a few more days, a few more days.

When the guests went to bed, Shoaib came by Aleema's side to help with the dishes.

"If you break your crockery, it will be our own loss. Not hers."

Aleema hmphed and started using a gentler hand.

"Just a few more days and she will be out of your hair. "

"You know it's not about that! It's her insolence, her refusal to lift a finger, and so many nakhke, ya Allah! You would think she's the queen of a country. Shoot me if I am ever this rude to anyone, let alone my own family."

Shoaib turned around, hoping no one heard. "Hush, she's my sister."

"So? Am I expected to cater to her every whim? First, she couldn't eat spicy food. Now she's become a vegetarian. If it's her lifestyle, why do I have to make the sacrifices? She can very well take care of herself and her son. Upar se, the other day, Nabeel was belittling Sayid for eating meat. I mean, what makes kids think they can judge others on their life choices! They literally just turned vegetarian a few months ago. How is it okay to let your kids talk down to anyone about food? "

"I agree to all of it. But we do it for family."

Aleema let out a laugh.

"Only *we* do it for the family. What about *them*?" Aleema gestured toward the guest bedroom.

"Ab jaane do. Let it go and go to bed. You will sleep easy. I will take care of the rest."

"I will sleep easy knowing I do the best I can. I don't know how she sleeps taunting and berating and making life hell for others and her son! Ouf!" Aleema threw the towel and headed to bed.

....

The next day, after work, Aleema served everyone chai and the kids snacks.

As she was about to sit with her own cup. "Oh! I don't think I can have chai in this heat today. Can you please give me some lemonade? "

Aleema looked at Shoaib and fumed. Through gritted teeth, she said, "Sayid, please get a glass of lemonade. "

Sayid dragged himself up and did the needful.

"Wonderful. It was so hot today, na. Haan, so what I was saying? I met Tahira today. She was inviting me to the Eid potluck they are hosting next week."

Aleema's chai froze mid-sip.

"Oh! Oops. She didn't invite you?" A smile played on her lips.

"No. But it's okay. I didn't expect her to." Aleema smiled.

Shafiqa's smile slipped. "Oh, okay. So she was telling me that for potluck, I can make my world-famous mutton biryani. I couldn't believe she would ask me that. I was straightforward. I just cannot do that. It's difficult for me. I am taking care of Nabeel also now alone while his dad is in Dubai, looking for a home. I just cannot. Once we have a home, maybe I will invite their family. But I certainly can't cook for twenty families. Who has the time and energy?"

Aleema felt the sun shining brighter on her.

The rest of the conversation drowned as Aleema went through her life and her parent's teachings of always helping others, no matter what.

Of putting the guest first and doing what you can for the family. And she realized, for the first time, not all rules apply to all people, and she deserves respect in her own home.

She came back to earth as Shoaib put a hand on hers and raised an eyebrow.

"Huh?"

"Aapa is asking something," Shoaib reiterated.

"Sorry, what?"

Shafika groaned with a hand to her head. "My allergies are flaring up while I sleep again. Can you please vacuum the bedroom today, before bedtime? Whenever you are free and have a minute. I just can't stand the dust. I don't imagine you are able to vacuum quite so frequently, what with work and all."

Aleema took a deep breath.

"Also, can you please make kaali daal for Nabeel today? I know you made chana for him. but he really wanted to have kali daal. "

Aleema smiled and stood up. "Appa, I would

love to, but it's really hard for me to cook two different kinds of meals every single day. Just today, ask him to manage, or you are welcome to cook in my kitchen any time. And Nabeel..." Nabeel looked up from where he was sitting on the floor. "Stop drawing on my walls."

Aleema picked up her cup and said, "I think today I will have chai in my room watching my favorite soap. Shoaib, vacuum is in the coat closet, behind the coats. "

With that, Aleema went into her room and shut the door.

PEACE

It's a reflex. To look up to thank the lady holding the door open for me, dusting the snow off myself. Mouthing a thank you, my eyes look beyond her.

The last person on earth I would ever want to see. My ex-boyfriend from seven years ago! What the hell is he doing here? He's staring at me, giving me that sheepish, disgusting smile I used to love.

He is probably cursing his own hard luck. Or

did he know I would be here?

Wait, why is he smiling? Does he not recognize me?

Sure, I've changed a lot. Seven years is a long time. What rubbish! Of course he does. God! I need to get out of *here*.

But the lady is already proudly good-jobbing her little kid for pressing floor number four, and the doors are shut.

My fate is quite literally sealed. I would only embarrass myself by running out of here.

He bends forward and presses twenty-one.

Panic, panic, panic!

Why did this damn building have to be twenty-five floors, and why is my office on the twenty-fourth? Has he got a job here? Will I have to see him every day? What is on the twenty-first floor? Law offices. He's not a lawyer, or has he become one? My hands are getting clammy. Is the air on in here?

Deep breath. Deep breath.

The fourth floor is here. Out they go.

Should I go out with them?

I will *not* give him the satisfaction. Besides, I don't want to climb sixteen floors! The laziness in me fights with my repulsion of him.

It's a matter of another minute or so. I can get through it with some dignity, I think?

Just him and me. *Was the elevator always so freaking small?*

That ceiling has so much dust on it. That corner even has a cob web. Does no one ever clean here?

Five... six... seven...

I should have saved myself this torture and got off when I had the chance.

Eight... nine... ten... eleven...

No, I'm stronger than that.

Twelve... thirteen...

Explicit expletives stream live through my dizzy head.

Fourteen... fifteen... sixteen...

Just a few more.

Seventeen...

Has this elevator always been so ridiculously slow as well?

Clang!

What was that? This is not happening. What are the chances of my two worst nightmares coming true at the same time? *Could this day get any worse?*

Deep breath. Deep breath.

I'm pressing the call button.

"Yes. How may I help you?"

"We are stuck on the seventeenth floor. Well, after, I guess."

"I'm sorry to hear that. Someone will be there

shortly."

I squeak out a thank you and think, "Hurry!" Don't look at him. *No, no, no!*

My breath comes in short spurts. My hands are sweating. Is my heart going to explode? I pull at the corners of the kameez and wring the dupatta within my hands.

"Ahem. I think you are having a panic attack. Have some water. Here."

Was he really talking, or are my ears ringing? I'm trying, but I can't see anything now. How dare he try to reach out? Everything seems to be fading out of focus.

I slap at his hand, extending the bottle.

"Brushing me off won't stop you from hitting the ground. Sit down."

Here, in this filthy elevator? My legs aren't supporting me anymore. Maybe the floor isn't so bad after all. I reach for the bottle, weakly sliding down into the lotus position. Opening the cap after a few pathetic tries, I take a few much-needed sips.

Deep breath. *One... two... three... four... five...*

"You seem well. I mean, you seemed well at least a few seconds ago. I'm sorry this is so awkward."

Ignore him. He will stop talking eventually.

"Are you okay?"

Deep breath. *Six... seven...*

"Can't we... for old time's sake at least..."

What is his problem?

"Well, this is ridiculous! It's not like we don't know each other. In fact..." *He* has the audacity to smirk!

I snap, "Can't we what? In what scenario is this okay? In what world do you think that you and I could be *anything*? It's been almost a decade of me trying not to think about..." Oh, God. My eyes are defying every single atom of my body and brimming up.

Defiance radiated off him. "I figure ... you... I... Well, time *has* passed."

"Time. Time is not magic. It simply buries everything till the problem comes back to stand right in front of you in an elevator that is not moving." I fume.

"Fine. Whatever. Nothing has changed. Ever the drama queen."

Did he freaking just roll his eyes at me?

I jump up and start punching the call button with all my hatred directed toward that one finger.

"Stop that. It will break."

"No, it will not."

"I'm talking about your finger!"

"Hello. Yes, how can I help you?" asks the service operator.

I plead. "Someone was supposed to come help. We are still stuck."

"Oh yes. I'm sorry. It seems like an electrical problem. We are working on it. The electrician will be here in half an hour, maybe earlier."

I close my eyes, and the tears roll down.

"Oh, really stop," he says, smirking in place. "I'm sure there are worse things than being stuck here with me. You forget we used to get along really well. It's just minutes, not a lifetime. Stop being such a baby," says the king of sarcasm.

Baby? Drama queen?

"Are you kidding me? True as that may be, it looks like you are still an asshole of enormous proportions!"

His eyes pop out. He regains his composure. "Colorful language coming from you. Looks like if nothing else, your vocabulary sure has extended. Though I'll have you know you weren't that great to be around either."

"Sure. But what was the tough part? Please enlighten me. Me being there for you at your beck and call, wanting to be with you? Sure, I was super clingy, but I was young. I was in love.

"I thought wanting to be with someone when you loved them was natural. What was tough for you, though? Me traveling every weekend to see you for a few hours? Or me being your personal punching bag, ever available to take every sarcastic remark you threw out?

"Or me spending all my money calling you, buying you stuff, visiting you. You didn't seem to mind any of that at all. In fact, you hardly ever even made any real effort for us, not even turning up to meet my parents when they were in town while I built my world around you.

Meanwhile, you went around flirting with every girl behind my back and lying about us to everyone around so that you were the quintessential eligible bachelor."

I'm panting. Years have disappeared at this moment...

Him looking sheepish was no relief. "Look! You left me. Got married, seem happy enough from what I know from social media. I am married, happily enough. We got what we wanted, I guess. So, why the angst? Aren't you happy?"

Tears are flowing freely. I smile through the tears. "Yes, I'm happy, married to a wonderful man. A man who surprisingly turned out to be everything you weren't."

"Hmph." He makes a face. Male ego, check.

I continue, "But every single time I think of you, I'm filled with regret. And questions. Was any of it real? I hate myself when I think about those years I *wasted* behind the vague idea of us. I don't care about you. Don't flatter yourself. But seeing you here reminds me of all those beautiful memories that only I thought were real, and love and trust that was all for nothing. Didn't I even deserve the respect of friendship? I hate myself for wasting my time, energy, money when I could have... I don't know; spent less years wondering *why I was not enough? Why didn't you want to put in the effort?* But later on, I understood that it wasn't me. As cliché as it is, it was actually all you! You didn't want to miss out on anything better if it chose to come around. All options open, as they say. And I guess you got it too. Just as you wanted. So, hurrah for us!" I throw my hands up in the air.

I sat back down, spent.

It's quiet. And it remains that way, thankfully.

Memories flooding us, our own versions of our truths haunting us with their ghosts.

All the good times, the laughter, the friendship, the intimacy, the fights, the pain, my begging him to change, my asking him to let me go, the abrupt end when I just stopped answering his calls after I found out he had been cheating on me, the ridiculousness of it all, even this moment here.

Why did I have to say anything? Why do I always talk so much? Does it even make any difference? But as the seconds tick away, I realize I do feel lighter. How come he's not saying anything? Maybe age does bring some maturity? Who knows. For the last five minutes, I felt like I was twenty-one again back at college, the stupid girl who believed in fairy tale romances.

Ten, twenty minutes have passed by. The red in my mind has passed. My mind wanders.

I wonder if the kids have had their lunches. What is my hubby going to say when I tell him about this surreal meeting?

I bet he will make some funny comment about how I finally got the last say I always love having. What am I going to make for dinner today? Baked chicken and beans, maybe.

And as I find myself coming back to the person I am now, I realize I'm actually fine. This, us here also seems fine. What are we but just two people who once were bound together by a different time and now aren't? Strangers.

I sigh in embarrassment as it hits me how futile and maybe foolish my outburst was. "I'm sorry. I really meant when I said it's not about you, and I realize now that this moment has passed, it's not even in me anymore. I shouldn't have said anything. But then I have read somewhere that when we meet someone from our past, we fall back into the ways of those old bygone times. Looks like it is true." I smile sheepishly. "I always talk too much for my own good."

He looks at me. For a second, he looks just like the person who was my friend. "It wasn't all lies, you know? I did love you. Maybe a part of me always will. I am sorry for being a jerk then."

I rub my sweaty hands on my kurta, smiling at the empty words, looking down. "Thank you."

Another long silence. The elevator dings and starts moving up to the twenty-first floor. I stand up. The doors open. He starts walking out. As the door closes, he looks back, smiles the smile

I used to say was the best one in the world, and waves bye.

———

A month later, I'm standing in the elevator and see that he's walking toward it again. He acknowledges me with a nod. I nod back. He turns around to face the doors. The elevator starts quietly, moving upward.

bias

"This is Madhu," Isha introduced the ladies at the restaurant. "Madhu, this is Seema, Pooja, Dhanvi, and Teesha."

They all smiled at each other.

"Are you new to the city?" Seema asked Madhu.

"No, just new to the neighborhood. We have been here for ten years now. "

"Wow! Practically an American, I guess," Dhanvi commented.

"Well, I was born here." Madhu smiled. "So I have always been an American."

Everyone looked at each other. After the long-standing H4 and EAD statuses they all had spent decades waiting for, someone being an American from birth was almost impressive. As if they had done something special to get the much-wanted status early.

"So, where are you from then?"

Madhu hid a smile. "Houston."

Dhanvi interjected. "She means where in India are you from?"

Madhu responded, looking at her glass, "I am not."

"Your parents, then?" Seema insisted.

"Oh! They are from India and South Africa."

The ladies looked at each other. For years, Madhu had experienced this with exasperation but now had grown to enjoy this part of introductions.

"So, do you speak Hindi or Gujarati?" Dhanvi asked.

"I speak Hindi fluently since Mom was a Mumbaiite. Dad learned Hindi while visiting India. I do understand Gujarati and Tamil."

"Oh! So you are Hindi speaking," Isha said, clapping her hands together. All the ladies nodded in approval. "Kudos to you for understanding Tamil. I don't get South Indians. They are constantly talking in that weird language, *kodokadai bandooputtu* types."

Madhu's smile fell. "My mom's heritage is Tamil. It's just that she was raised in Mumbai. "

Isha went through a few shades of pink, flustering. "Oh! I don't mean to be rude. It's just that their language is so difficult to understand, na. And they never think about who is around them."

Teesha jumped in. "Haan toh, we are all in America now. But people should think about where they are when they speak in their own language. We are all from different parts of India, coming here. I am from Gujraat. Isha is from Gujraat too, and Seema was raised in Dubai."

Madhu smiled tightly. "That's nice. How long have you been in the states?"

Seema replied, "I came to graduate and have been here since."

Hmm. Everyone took a sigh of relief, moving on to the safe topic of graduation in the United States and life after.

Madhu rolled her eyes inwardly as the conversation shifted gradually into Gujarati. She waited a while for a break in the conversation.

"Umm, I would really appreciate you all sticking to Hindi or English. I don't really understand that dialect all that well. Or if you would be so kind as to translate."

Everyone looked at each other blankly.

Isha responded, "I didn't realize. I thought you said you understand Gujraati. Your hubby is... so we... I thought..."

"Yeah, it happens a lot. But there are many dialects in Gujraati. I don't get the one you all are speaking."

Madhu felt everyone inwardly wincing, irritated, she was sure. She smiled to break the tension. "I get why you would think that. Happens all the time. His family, friends. Even when we were getting married, his family also thought it would be a good fit. Jokes on them.

Nervous laughter all around.

"I am used to it. Just a few translations here and there. No biggie."

"Of course, of course," Isha said. "Not a problem at all. Seema, speaking of in-laws, didn't yours just buy a home? How is it going?" And the conversation resumed.

Madhu smiled and nodded, knowing full well that within the next fifteen minutes, everyone would be back to speaking Gujraati. She guessed she may not be invited back for girl's night any time soon.

judgement

The sky was a dull ivory color, clouds above threatening every few minutes.

Radha pulled back the curtain further and looked out. She folded her hands across her chest as she took in the might of the vista before her. Great.

Even the skies denied her hope.

From this point, it looked like the world was conspiring against her. She had to do what she had to do. The wheels had been set in motion when she'd opened her eyes this morning to the phone ringing.

Mo had not left her with much of a choice. Theirs had always been a complex relationship. She groaned out loud.

She'd noticed by her own and the experiences of those around her that love always complicated things a hell lot before simplifying them any. It had been love at first conversation for Mo, but she, the practical one, had always maintained a distance.

After a few months of trying to whisk her away on an official date, she had relented, and things had spiraled out of control immediately, going way too fast. His feelings were obvious from the get-go, and as relationships at the workplace tended to get, the sparks and tongues were soon flying. They were incompatible in every way, but he was so sure of everything that soon she found herself pulled into his fantastical web. Stupidly yes, but the exhilaration made her feel so powerful, she remembered guiltily.

The more they got to know one another, the more their differences became apparent, and within the turmoil, they often found euphoria. If only she had stopped much earlier, then it wouldn't have come to this.

But she hadn't, and now someone might just get hurt. She wrung her hands in despair. She'd always known a time would come when she'd have to face the music for her pieces of silver. Didn't we all always have bad days right after good ones?

She had never imagined it would be so soon. Mo had been given an opportunity to head a project in Switzerland.

And she was in the crosshairs of the decisions.

He wanted her with him, and she didn't know how she was going to handle the matter.

She was sure it was too soon to commit, and he was equally sure that they were meant to be. He was impulsive, childish, an eternal romantic. She wasn't. He was so many things she wasn't, and yet the one trait they shared was stubbornness.

She shuddered at the thought of the call in

the morning. She'd woken up at 5:15 a.m. with the insistent ringing of her cell.

"Are you going to come or not?"

"What? Mo? Do you know what time it is?"

"I waited as long as I could. Now I can't anymore. Are you going to come or not?"

She pulled herself up in her bed, composing her mind. "Why don't you understand? It's not that easy to just get up and decide such things so suddenly. "

"Yes, it is! It's a simple enough question. Do you love me enough? If you know that, then we can work things out. I won't go if that's what it takes. " He sounded so earnest that her heart broke.

"Have you slept at all?"

"Don't change the subject."

"Okay! What do you want me to say? Don't go? But you have to. It's a chance of a lifetime. I would never let such an opportunity pass me by. I want what's best for you. Besides, you've worked so hard for this. You have to go. "

"So you want me to go, and you aren't willing to say that you'll try, even? I get it."

"It's not that cut and dry, and you know it. You're not being fair. It's just that..."

"I know everything there is to know. But I'm all in, so the ball is in your court. You have until tonight to tell me what you've decided. Either way, I'll be right here, waiting. Either you come, or I am not going." And he'd cut the call, just like that.

He left her staring at the receiver, aghast at the ultimatum. She'd tried calling him back, but he never picked up, even cutting her calls a few times. She didn't blame him. She had dilly-dallied long enough, even by her standards, and the excuses that she'd been putting forward seemed lame, even to her ears now.

She just had to take her courage in her hands and put her play into the game. She looked at the moon through the clouds and wished she was as sure of her place in the universe.

She'd taken sick leave, taking a long, exhausting

walk alone thinking about every possible scenario, and she had decided. She still had no idea about what she wanted, but at least now, she was absolutely sure about what she did not want.

She turned away from the window and walked toward the phone, all her fears and uncertainties of tomorrow causing her to shiver.

She picked up her cell and dialed. It rang a few times, and the call connected.

She spoke firmly. “Hello...

“...How are you?...

“...I’m okay...

“...Uh, Papa, I’m coming over tomorrow. I needed to talk to you and Mummy...

“...No, I need to do this face to face...

“...I’m sorry, it can’t wait...

“...I said no, I will talk tomorrow...

“...Um... It would be good to wait till tomorrow...

"...You're being childish... Well, it's about this guy at work...

"...No, he's not harassing me, yaar...

"...Yes, Papa. I know you could still manage to break his bones if he did...

"...Great, you both are on speaker!

"...Stop yelling! He wants to marry me...

"...Hello?! Hello?

"...No, Yes, I want to marry him too...

"...No, he's not from our caste...

"...No, he doesn't speak Marathi either. He's from Delhi...

"...Mom, please don't get melodramatic. I know you didn't want it like this, but he's a really good person, and he loves me...

"...You saw him at our office party when you were visiting...

"...Yes, that's him...Yes, he is tall...

"...Ummmm...

"...Yes, those were his friends who helped Shalu prep for that job interview...

"...Um...

"...He is not Hindu...

"...Mom, stop crying... It just happened..." She was also crying now.

"...I can understand, but you cannot hate him before meeting him, right?

"...That is ridiculous...The world is way ahead of casteism, religion...Urgh... I told you to let me come and talk to you...

"...He loves me a lot...

"...No, I won't be converting...

"...Yes, we have talked about it..."

The next question made her laugh. "Abhi, what kids and all! We will teach our kids what we teach them, and they can choose... God is God, right?

"...Sure, you can take the kids to temples when and if they are born...
Yes, you can sing bhajans to them..." She rolls her eyes.

"...Just more than a year...

"...Now because he got promoted to VP of Operations last week and has to move to Germany within the next two, three months and he wants me to go with him...

"...He's more qualified than me, yes...

"...Family? Dad's into banking, mom is a teacher, and he's got a sister... in college...

"...Ummm... Yeah...

"...Okay, I'll tell him to meet us for lunch...

"...No, he's not very picky about food... Brinjal, I guess...

"...Yes, Ma, I'm sure...

"...No, I'll remember the bone breaking thing... Yes, I'll tell him...

"...Yes, there are worse choices I could have made... whatever that means...

"...Thank you, thank you, thank you! See you tomorrow... Love you both." She clutched the phone to her chest as her eyes brimmed with tears and her lips widened into a smile of relief.

She'd actually thought there would be violence, but her parents had shocked her. Wow. Now she knew that they loved her enough to want her to be happy, no matter how they truly felt.

Thank God, for her mind was now made up, and nothing would change it.

She re-dialed. The call connected on the first ring.

"Hello? Sitting next to the phone *kya*? Anyway, I've decided. I'm all in too..." She laughed out loud at the response. "Of course, I'll marry you, silly! I love you too... Oh, by the way, lunch tomorrow at my parent's place. It's a two-hour drive. Pick me up at 10 a.m. Oh, and don't forget to wear a thick shirt."

And she cut the call. Let him sweat a while, just

a little. Radha giggled to herself in anticipation of the days ahead.

belief

"How was school today, Reva?"

"It was okay."

"You don't look okay."

"It was fine, Ma."

I wonder what's eating her? Maya fretted inside while trying to be calm outside. "Did someone say something?"

"No."

Down to monosyllables is not a good sign. Reva is usually quite talkative. "How was your day, Rahul?" Maya turned to her son, who was munching on roti daal. Between bites, he mumbles, "Was fine. Miss Samantha gave us a test in math."

"How did you do?"

"Fine."

Maya tried hard not to roll her eyes. Reva being three years older than Rahul meant he picked up on her habits. You would think at eleven and eight, she could get more out of her kids.

"Okay. After food, make sure you guys finish your homework, then in the evening, we have to go for the Kanchak rounds."

"What's that?"

"The one where they take blessings from young girls and give them gifts, the night before Navratri."

"It's not fair," whined Rahul.

"Some aunties will give you something also. It's just a traditional celebration of girls."

Reva picked her plate and took it to the kitchen. Rahul looked at her and then their mom and shrugged.

As the evening came, Maya got dressed in her salwar kurta and went to Reva's room. She pushed open the door to see Reva sleeping. "Why aren't you ready?!" Maya exclaimed.

"I don't want to."

Maya sits down with her daughter. "What's going on, beta? Someone said something to you?"

Reva pulls her knees up and pulls the sheet to her chest. "No one said anything. I just don't want to go."

"Aise nahi karte betu. We were invited. It's a blessing to go. And all you have to do is take prasad and come home. You don't have to eat there either. We just have three homes to go to today. Meena and Shaila were busy, so they dropped your prasad in the morning."

Reva scrunched her face up in anger, "I. Don't. Want. To. Go!"

Maya tussles her hair. "So much anger."

Reva bursts out crying and rushes out the door to the restroom next to her room. Maya's eyes follow her daughter's exit, worrying about the millions of things that could have gone wrong.

Did someone comment about her curly hair or about her being chunky again? Did her friends ignore her at lunch again? Did she not have any company during soccer practice? Did her teacher ignore her during questions again? Did she do badly on a test? Did someone try to tease her, or worse... Touch her? Did someone send her an inappropriate text?

Involuntarily, Maya turned to pick up her daughter's phone when she noticed the stain on the sheet.

Okay! Deep breathes, thought Maya. We have talked about this. She knows what to do. It's fine; she's fine. It's just new! Poor baby.

While Reva was in the restroom, Maya changed the sheets and got Reva a glass of juice, some snacks, and a bar of chocolate. When Reva comes out of the restroom, Maya hands her the chocolate bar. “I thought we had agreed you would tell me. Is it hurting a lot?”

“No! Not really.” Reva rubs the back of the neck with the palm of her hand.

“When did they start?”

“Last night. I used the pad in the bathroom.”

Maya was surprised. She would have thought Reva would have told her.

“Do you have any questions?”

“Not right now, no.”

“Then what’s wrong, darling? It’s totally natural to feel weird about it. I have had my periods for twenty-five years now, and I am still not used to them.”

Reva whispers, “Yeah, it’s weird. My tummy is hurting a little, and my back.”

Maya starts massaging Reva’s back. “Yeah, every single body is different. Your symptoms we will know as time passes. I will give you something for that pain now. Is that why you are upset?"

"No, it's not that."

"What is it then?"

"I am not wanted at the Kanjak now, right? You said it's for little girls, considered pure." Reva adds air quotes with her fingers. "I am mature now, right?"

"I will miss out on the halwa puri and all and meeting everyone." Her hands slumped down.

"Oh!" Maya was at a loss for words. She waited a few seconds to think of a response. "Hmmm. I don't think anyone is mature at 11." Maya did air quotes too, with a smirk. She shrugged her shoulders. "But I don't know what everyone thinks about it. Traditionally, yes, girls are not invited if they have had their periods."

Reva's eyes looked down, and she picked up her stuffy. She noticed the changed bedsheets and smiled at her mom.

Maya wondered what to do.

"Does this mean I can't do Laxmi Puja tomorrow?"

"Dhaattt! I don't believe in all this. For me, Laxmiji is a woman herself, and being able to have babies is the most beautiful thing in the world. Besides..." Maya shifted to the bed, putting her hand around her daughter. "In our little four-person family, how can we enjoy Laxmi Puja without you, our little Laxmi? "

Maya poked a finger in her daughter's tummy playfully.

"I hate having my periods, but having you and Rahul in my life is a blessing from Goddess Laxmi herself."

"Is this why you don't do Kanjak puja?"

"Hmmm... yeah. I don't want to offend anyone. I would love to feed a bunch of kids, but it's hard to say no to boys or girls who are now getting their periods earlier and earlier."

"Ah! I always wondered." Reva placed a hand on her mom's leg.

"Besides, these rules of women being

separate, not praying during these days, and staying away from the kitchen were all right for the times when they were followed. It was the only way women would get any rest on these hard days. Now, I don't think it applies so much to our world. But then again, we still have to respect others' who still believe. Maybe they have another reason why they still follow these practices."

Reva nodded.

Maya smiled. "Okay! Let me text the aunties and let them know that we won't be coming. "

Rahul popped his head in then, leaning against the door frame, his hands on the side of the door. "What? You aren't even going? Not even to Devaki aunty's house? She always sends extra prasad and a gift for me. Why do bad things only happen to me?" He stomped out.

Maya called to Rahul, "Rahul! Get me my phone."

"No!"

"*Acha bacha*. Good boy. Go get it. Then I will get you ice cream, and we can all have a movie night."

"Okay." While Rahul ran to Maya's bedroom and got the phone, Reva put her head down on Maya's lap and closed her eyes.

"Here." Maya took the phone and messaged her friends personally. "Please excuse us from attending Kanjak today. I am not sure it would be right for us to come. Think of us in your prayers." The messages got the blue ticks almost instantly. Maya threw the phone down on the bed with a thud.

Maya shuddered, feeling bad for her little girl, who loved this festival. Shaking it off, she smiled. "There! Now you rest, and I will go make puri halwa chana for you both, and then we can have that ice cream I promised. "

Maya was almost up when her phone rang. It was Devaki calling. "Hello... Yeah... Just today... She's fine, overall... No, no pain... Oh! Really. But I thought... Nahi, it's okay, you carry on, dear... You are so sweet, but what if someone... Oh okay... Thank you. She will be so happy."

Reva looked at her, questioning. Maya patted her daughter on her back. "Chalo, get ready.

Devaki aunty has asked both of you to come over. We can pick up ice cream on the way back."

Rahul jumped in the air. "Yay!" Reva tapped him on his head, hard. "It's a festival for girls. Why are you so happy?"

Rahul grinned and said impishly, "Didn't you hear? Times have changed." Maya's mouth remained open as the kids laughed heartily.

respect

“On my way.”

She sighed, looking at the text. Her shirt was stuck to her body. She could barely breathe. It was so hot.

The sun was turning her red, inside and out. With every passing minute, her frustration was mounting. It had been forty-five minutes, probably more.

How many times in the past year had she found herself standing at this very bus stop in the heat, bearing stares of passers-by, even lewd looks?

She was sick of it. She looked around searchingly, hoping that she would see him come around the corner. Another bus came and passed her by. She scanned for his familiar face in the midst of strangers and looked away instantly in fear that her curiosity would be mistaken for interest. Men!

This was not unusual. Whenever they were to meet, it was the same. She waited for him. He took his sweet time coming and then made some lame excuse about why he was late.

"Mom wanted me to get groceries."

"Dad wanted me to go with him to someone's house to pick something up."

"My sister needed a ride to her classes."

Then why didn't he inform her about the delay? And a couple of times, he had just fallen asleep. What were phones even for?

Desi boys and their secret lives. Too cool to not have a girlfriend, too scared of their parents to tell them about her.

Each time she was left aghast at his callousness in regard to her. She adapted by coming late, and he adapted by coming later.

Many times before, she knew she should have just left. She would be sticky with sweat, and her legs would start aching, but she'd keep waiting in case he came within the next few minutes, and she was worried she'd miss him by a second or two.

It wasn't just this. Nothing was right, she fretted. But they were in love. Wasn't love supposed to make everything right? In love, every little or big hindrance is overcome and cherished. Isn't it?

Then why was it that with each passing day, she felt she was the only one trying to pull their bond forward, like a donkey carrying a load too big for it?

She couldn't remember the last time when she had been truly happy. Sure, they had their happy and loving and true moments. And the passion... the passion was through the roof. Just looking at him would make her melt.

But was that enough?

He was passing snide, hurtful comments that she could brush under the rug. And if she didn't, they would have massive fights that would leave her in tears, and then they wouldn't speak for a few days.

He said he loved her. He did even care for her. She could see it in the way he would get her favorite treats or help out her friends when they needed it. She sighed again, thinking back to the time when she was really upset. He had to leave her birthday party, but he came back later, just to surprise her. Seeing him make that effort had filled her with joy.

But was that enough?

They weren't even married. What would it be like later? Why did the love they share leave her feeling hollow instead of valued? A tear rolled down her face again.

She looked across the road to where he'd magically appeared.

55 minutes late.

He raised his hand in mock salute with no expression for remorse, with a smile that always made her heart skip a beat. Now, it just left her wondering why he didn't care about her enough to value her time. But even if he knew she was in love, he also knew that she'd forgive him for anything.

She looked at him as he came toward her, noticing a bus coming from the corner of her eye. As the bus stopped, she climbed into it, turning back to give a short wave to the face which her life had been revolving around till that moment.

A face that was now full of questions.

She giggled as she saw him throwing his hands up in exasperation. Deciding at that moment that she deserved better, she was liberated of her own chains, finally. Now, coming back to this bus stop depended on whether someone was willing to wait for her...

cruelty

He held her close. Her essence blended into him.

He wanted to hold her so tight that they would become one forever. He breathed her in, and all the moments they spent together flashed before his eyes. He kissed her face, snuggling her in, just the way she liked it.

The first time they met, as she walked across that college campus. That first time they had chai together under the tapri with those pakodas.

Their wedding day was attended by a million people they didn't know. Flying to the US and figuring out the cultural differences together. Time had been kind to them, letting them discover friendship and love together.

The memories of every meeting passed through his being, and he smiled, looking into her face. Her beautiful face, with her beatific smile, her luscious hair that so softly shaped around her face, and her brown, sharp eyes that never missed a thing, kind, loving, seeing into your soul, and always smiling.

The eyes into which he always looked for inspiration to live, eyes that told him she loved him unconditionally and with all her being.

Eyes that were today dead to the world...

Yes, time had been kind to them, but why has it been so cruel now? Her cycle lay on the road, as twisted as his insides.

The crowd surrounding them on the road collectively took a step back, not letting go of their phones, as a howl of fury escaped his lips and tears came rushing down his face.

perception

I hazily reached for the alarm. Oh, wait! Was this the alarm or the door?

I squinted toward the door to the bedroom and dragged myself out to open it. Daylight was just breaking outside, and the doorbell rang again. Cursing, I opened the door to the biggest bouquet of roses I'd ever seen.

The delivery guy handed me the flowers. I glowed from within, thinking, "What a way to start my day!" Slamming the door shut with my foot, I ran to place the flowers in a vase and, with equal fervor, dialed the number I spoke to last night.

I yelled into the mouthpiece, "I love you. I love you. I love you. Thank you so much. You made my day. It's the first-ever time I've gotten such a lavish bouquet."

The energy at the other end was in total contrast to mine. "Wha—Who?"

"Thank you for the flowers you sent me. Red and white, just the way I like them."

"Sharvari? Is that you?" And then, with a smile. "Happy Birthday, sweetheart. You've got flowers?"

"Yes, dummy," I said, laughing. "The ones you sent?"

"Well, as much as I'd love to take credit for them, I can't. I just flew in yesterday, remember? I didn't get the time. But do let me know who they are from. I'm not gone a week, and someone's already wooing you?"

Perplexed, I reached for the card and opened it.

"To a precious joy that brightens my world many, many happy returns of the day!"

On the phone, I said, "It doesn't say."

"Looks like someone's trying to impress you," said the jealous guy.

And I think it's creepy. I don't want flowers from anyone other than my boyfriend, "I know this is just like you. Pretty expensive prank. So, it would be better for you to admit it so I can thank you in kind." I smirked at my end.

"Like I said, I can't take credit for it. The only reason is I don't want someone else coming up and asking you about them, making me look like a fool. You know it's not in my nature for me to turn down an exciting offer like that." He laughed.

I giggled like a schoolgirl. " Pervert! And I love you for it. Okay, so we have a mystery for today. Probably someone being extra nice. I still think it's you, though."

"Well, I'm lucky my reputation as a prankster precedes common sense. I'm going back to sleep now, you have a good day. I'll come to your place after work, and then you and I can have dinner together, right?"

"Right." I made kissing sounds into the phone. I still think he's just messing with me.

....

We met on the train, both on our way to work, fresh out of college with an eye on the future. And after a small chat about why I couldn't give him my number, I agreed to meet him for coffee. Coffee turned to dinner, which turned into endless days together, and here we were, two years later. Last year we felt our way carefully, getting to know each other better. It was only in the present year that we both seemed to be getting serious, to the point of predicting the next argument.

Life seemed pleasant enough, except we both were working hard at making a name in our respective careers. We were in that position where people our age are not too wealthy yet to splurge on things, which is why we're always making those ends meet.

Vaibhav Banerjee, working on a new company that he'd started with two other friends and me,

Sharvari Singh, a quality analyst at Roots, a mobile company.

...

My day had already taken off on a high note. On the other hand, if the flowers were from a psycho lusting after me, I'd be pretty disappointed.

I got dressed and went to work. I got wishes all day long, but no hint at the person who sent the flowers.

Vaibhav even called during the day to ask if I'd found out who sent the flowers and if I'd seen anything suspicious happening during the past few days or weeks. To say the least, I was getting more and more worried by the minute. What kind of creep does this thing? I was going to trash those flowers when I got back home. Disappointing, but it's the principle of the thing.

Evening came, and in walked Joan, my friend from the days when I was in pigtails. "How's it going, birthday girl? Here's my contribution for today," she said in her sing-song voice, handing me a gift.

I hugged her. “Thank you, sweetheart. Where would I be without your charity?” I teased.

She raised an eyebrow. “Without me, you’d probably still be in a ponytail dressing like a nun.”

I let the comment slide, as there is always some truth to what Joan says. Being a totally in-vogue lady, she would die before being seen with someone who didn’t seem well put together.

“Okay, Miss Fashion Police. How do I look today?”

“Hmm, the hoop earrings and white lace top go well with your trousers, but don’t you think you ought to get a little frilly for the celebrations tonight? And once again, I come to the rescue. Do open my present, darling!”

Grinning, I removed the wrapping, and out fell an elegantly cut, knee-length, off-shoulder crimson dress. Raising an eyebrow, I smirked. “Lucky is my middle name!”

“Well, I tried talking you into something that time we went shopping together, but since you wouldn't hear of buying something new for your birthday, I obliged."

I hugged her tight. "Jo's way or highway... It's lovely, and at the risk of further inflating your balloon-sized ego, your taste is impeccable, as always. So, shall we leave?"

"Yes, let's! I am dying to go back to your place and spend a quite dull, boring evening with you and Vaibhav, playing the third wheel under protest. I do wish you'd have a party once in your life, and let us all have a good time. After all, we all could always use an excuse to celebrate."

Exasperated, I flung my hands upward. "For the billionth time, it's my birthday, and I like spending it this way, with two people special to me with food delivered to my doorstep. You do know it's not that I'm averse to parties. It's just that finding the time to organize something is such an ordeal. And it's especially hard getting all the people I'd like to have, into one place, at the same time. Only last week, I asked Tony and Devi to join us, and they already had other plans for today."

Jo mumbled, "Yeah, yeah, yeah. I know the drill.

Let's just move on."

Walking toward the station, I remembered the bouquet. " Hey, did you send me flowers this morning?"

The surprised look on her face told me I'd hit the wrong number again. "What flowers?" She elbowed me in the waist with an exaggerated few winks.

"Oh, it's nothing. I just got a lavish bouquet of flowers in the morning. Really pretty, just the kind of flowers I like too. Only the card doesn't say who it's from. Naturally, I assumed it was from V, but then he said he didn't send them. I've been trying to figure it out since morning. Any ideas?"

She rolls her eyes. "There's a pickle, isn't it? Well, let me think. Hey! How about that cool English guy you met at that conference? You told me he seemed really into you."

"Henry? Well, for one thing, I haven't seen him in months. Though, he still sounds almost on the verge of dropping hints about wanting to go out with me when he texts with those winky emoji and coffee GIFs. But nothing over-the-top.

Besides, how would he know about my birthday or the kind of flowers I like?"

"You never know who turns out to be totally crazy about you, or psychotic for that matter." She smirked.

"Yeah, thanks for making me feel all better," I retorted.

"Okay, sorry, sorry. Let's just drop it. For all you know, it might have come to the wrong address on a fluke."

"That would be wonderful at this point." I smiled ruefully.

"I'm feeling thirsty. How about a drink? And we know for a fact that V is going to be late. We might as well take advantage of that."

"Hey! Give him a break. He's not that bad. It's a special day. You never know," I said in his defense, helplessly.

"Yeah, right. The day V comes on time is the day pigs will fly. I swear, either he doesn't own a watch or doesn't know how to tell time. C'mon! Just one drink. I know this nice place is ten minutes from here. And I promise we'll be outta there in fifteen, twenty minutes. My treat. Don't you want me to be hydrated?"

Sad but true. V had many qualities, but there was just something wrong with the way he calculated the time taken to reach from point A to point B.

I lamented on. "It's the only truly Desi thing about him. He runs on IST, Indian Standard time. I think it's' partly the coffee breaks he loves taking all the time.It's the same every time I go to India. No matter what the time, everyone is ready for chai, and then everyone collectively gets late because, of course, chai means there have to be samosas, kachoris, farsaan, or something with it. And then chai is not something one has on the go. So everyone keeps chatting. It's soooo irksome. With him, I think it's those coffee breaks, five-six times a day. "

Jo laughs, "You sound like how I feel about your boyfriend."

I grin as she pulls my hand in the direction she wants to take me.

"You'll love this place. I've been meaning to

take you to it for so long, but I'm glad we're going today."

As we continued walking, my mind trailed away to the many options for takeaway and movies for the night.

Thinking of food and movies brought me to the fact that it was my birthday and another eventful year had passed by. It always amazes me how meeting someone completely alien to you can become a part of every moment of your life. Sure, V wasn't perfect, but then neither was I. Somedays, I really hoped that things would grow to something more, but then I didn't want to rush anything so, it's just up to fate again to show me how far our love blooms.

Speaking of blooming, I really wonder who sent those flowers. I hadn't thought about Henry, but it couldn't be. On the other hand, it's just the kind of extravagant gesture he would make. After skillfully avoiding his charming advances at the conference, I'd agreed to have coffee and purposefully mentioned V and how I'm a one-man woman. Still, if not for V, nothing would have come of Henry and me. He was just not my type, so to speak.

Then who could it be sending flowers to me? Probably one of my sweet pals pulling a fast one on me or a freak accident. I'd feel sorry for the girl who missed out on those flowers, though. They were to die for. Just right in every way...

"Hey! Earth to Queen of the Milky Way... What Are you thinking about?" I was brought back to attention by Jo's snapping fingers.

"Nothing. Just wondering about those flowers."

"Well, nothing like a nice mystery man to make life worth living! That wheatish golden complexion you have, those bouncy waves, kohled eyes. Throw around your youth to attract as many men as you can. Once you get married, it all goes down the drain," said the ever-wise yet deeply dark Joan.

I smiled and let her lead me into the semi-dark restaurant. I could hardly see a thing and had just begun to wonder why Jo would get me to a place that makes me feel blind. " Jo, what is this place?"

"The ambiance is romantic, sweetie. It's a cozy place to forget all your worries; that's what it is. You know what? Let's go to the top. The view is to die for.

You'll love it."

I was hesitant. "I don't know, Jo. It was going to be just a drink or two. V might be waiting."

She pulled my hand, laughing. "C'mon! You know as well as I do he won't. Let's have some fun. Let me make this birthday special for you."

I knew better than to try to argue with her. V wasn't Jo's favorite person in the world. They both were cordial to each other at best, as Jo thought I could do much better. One of the main reasons again was that many times I ended up alone or waiting for him everywhere. I didn't blame him, as we always worked around things, but I certainly loved her for caring as much as she did. I smiled and tagged along. It was worth it, just to see the smile that lit up her face.

We entered the elevator and went up to the twentieth floor. As we got out of the lift, all I saw was darkness, and then there was a blast of...

"Surprise!"

I jumped with fright and, to say the least, I got the shock of my life when the lights came on. I saw everyone I've ever cared for smiling back at me. The group seemed to be limited magically to all the people I would have called if I was arranging the party by myself. And in the middle of them all, right at the back, was V. He was standing on a chair, grinning from ear to ear. Everyone started singing, "Happy birthday to you!"

I laughed like I'd never laughed before. The music started, and the lights went dark and then totally goofy. I greeted everyone around me, smiling, accepting everyone's wishes, my heart glowing with love for everyone I saw. My eyes were searching and looking at Jo and V, with a special smile for them and a number of questions in my twinkling eyes.

Once everyone had wished me, I walked up to them and hugged them both tight like there was no tomorrow... "What have you been up to? This is too much."

Jo giggled. "See, I told you this would be a special birthday. Your eyes are positively twinkling. I'm so happy to see you didn't have a heart attack."

I laughed, turning to V. "And you! What do you have to say for yourself? Conniving monster."

"Well, birthday girl, I just wanted to see your face experience something you thought you wouldn't enjoy."

"I must admit, it's incredible. I can't imagine how you guys had the time to plan all of this." I pointed at Jo. "You, with your assignments..." I looked at Vaibhav. "You with all your upcoming contracts and running around. And you actually timed everything perfectly, hiding everything from me. And I know more about your routine than you..."

Jo looked at V affectionately, which was a shocker in itself, and said, "Well, it's been a lot of hard work from this guy here. It was all his idea. Though I was in from the moment he said the word 'party'. We had to synchronize with everyone and make sure everyone we knew could come."

I felt my eyes well up. "Oh my God... That's so sweet, you guys! Thank You so much."

Vaibhav held my hand and pulled me closer. "You deserve it, sweetheart!" He pulled a rose magically out of thin air. "Don't let go of this one."

I took it and smiled into his eyes. "I wouldn't dream of it."

The evening seemed to fly by that night. Everyone seemed to be having a blast. Jo had arranged a number of games which were all fun, though a tad embarrassing. The rest of the time, everyone was just having a time dancing their feet off. The gifts just seemed to be flying in.

So were roses and flowers from Vaibhav. Every once in a while, someone would present me with a flower of a different color, or he would come along with a rose.

Each stem brought a smile to my face and a look from him that just melted my already full heart. Before I knew it, my hand had twenty-five roses.

As I finished talking to another flower bearer, I felt a tap on my shoulder. "Peek-a-boo!" Turning around, I smiled. "Oh! It's you." We laughed.

"Another one for my princess, and this time it's a pretty pink one for the pink I see in her sweet lips."

I took the new addition to my ever-growing bouquet. “Thank you, my prince. Please enlighten me on the reason for this shower of petals.”

He stood straight and bent at his waist in a princely way. “How is one to see his woman being wooed by another? It hurt my sentiments today when I learned that there was another fighting me for the affections of my princess.”

It took a moment for the words to sink in as I remembered the elaborate bouquet decorating my living room, and I laughed out loud. “You’ve got to be kidding. “ I looked at him aghast. “Sweetie? Tell me you’re not serious. Vaibhav?”

He looked down and shrugged sheepishly. “ I just... I just... I don’t know. You sounded so excited when you saw those flowers, I...”

I was aghast. I never thought something like this would make him jealous. Though kind of silly, it was a sweet sight to see. “Sweetheart, that’s ridiculous. No one can compare to you.” I reached for his hand. “I love you. Nothing can replace that, certainly not flowers that come out of nowhere.” Spreading one hand around his, I said, “Besides, you’ve certainly compensated for those flowers a million times over today.”

"You shouldn't have taken them then If they meant nothing." He looked almost upset.

"Well, I assumed they were from you," I elaborated.

"Well, I was busy working and putting together all this. I'm sorry if I wasn't the first one to wish you a happy birthday. You should be glad someone made your morning," said Mr. Grumpy.

"This is absurd. You know I don't care about such things. I know you're busy with work and all. And it's silly that you gave me all these flowers in competition with someone you don't even know. Hell, I don't even know!"

He looked at me pointedly. "Don't you? Is there something you wanna tell me?"

I was shocked. This was ridiculous. "No, V! There is nothing I want to tell you."

"What about that Henry fellow?"

"What about him? Puh-lease. I hardly know the guy."

"Well, you always say good things about him

and those texts, and he didn't even bother showing up when Jo invited him."

I rolled my eyes. "I couldn't care less about whether he comes or not. And he's good at his job. You are being childish right now."

"Childish, is it?" I don't think someone who prances around at the sight of flowers has a right to call me childish."

"V!" Keeping my temper in check, I hissed as tears filled my eyes. "Can you for once listen to yourself?! I don't care about those stupid flowers. I care about you. I thought they were from you, else I would have never accepted them. If it means that much to you, I'll throw them out the window right now."

I started walking away when he pulled me back to him.

Suitably chastised, he blinked, shaking his head. "I'm sorry. I don't know what came over me. No, you needn't go and throw them away. I am sorry... I did all this for you, and look, I made you cry. I'm so sorry, love! Can you forgive me?" After a pause, he said tentatively, "... and throw them out later?"

A laugh escaped me. He was totally exasperating, and I loved even that about him. "Sure! Anything that makes you happy.." I smiled and squeezed his shoulder. "I love you, you big, silly, stubborn oaf!"

"I love you too, you sweet, beautiful, caring, forgiving gem."

I didn't know whether to laugh or cry. I chose to just smile and went over to dance with friends.

As the evening flowed, there were the flowers that kept coming, making me look like I was going to open a flower shop shortly. I'd even begun to work on the tagline for my imaginary shop. Finally, I found my arms straining under the weight, and yet, I couldn't bring myself to put them down.

My parents called me over. My dad chided me. "That is one hell of a boy. I was surprised when Jo told me about him wanting to give you a party. And this evening, I see he's a little too free with his love for you. I wish you two would get married already.."

I blushed. "Dad, he's just being sweet. Now, don't start about where or how things are going.

I like the way things are for now."

Mom touched and smelled the flowers. "Well, he has to be quite serious to go through so much trouble... And he is absolutely charming. He's been taking exceptional care of us since we came in yesterday."

I didn't know what to say. I walked away on the pretense of being called away. Walking over to the window, looking at the city lit up below, I could only think of all the beauty in the world being brought unto me. No one thought of or planned for the future more than me, but I wasn't one to push someone into marriage. I believed if it was meant to happen, it would. But this information was new. Totally out of character, this evening's festivities would have taken a lot of effort. With his work and trips, I can only imagine what he must have gone through to put everything together. And the flowers! It was so sweet, but everything must have cost him a fortune. A silly thing to do just to win my feelings over, not that it's possible with just flowers, I thought with a smile. But it was the thought that counted! Truth be told, till the moment his outrageous outburst surprised me, I'd fully expected them to be from him. Well! It wasn't him. Then who?

"Penny for your thoughts?" Jo came to stand by me.

"It's all just so perfect. I feel it's a dream from which I never want to wake up."

"Yes! My presence does have that effect on people. But you are the first girl to feel that way."

We giggled. "You are amazing, you know that?"

"Well, darling, unfortunately for most people, I am aware of that. So, you like?"

She looked so innocent, asking how I liked the party, that I had to grin. "Time of my life, baby!"

She kissed my cheek. "And then some more..."

"So, thank you! I'd honestly forgotten how much fun birthdays could be."

"Don't thank me. Thank Vaibhav. I just did some of the footwork and a lot of the call making, which is my favorite hobby anyway. The real genius behind it was V. He truly came into my good books with all the thought he put into this, wanting everything to be perfect and all.

Though he can be a slave driver when he puts his mind to it."

I brimmed with pride.

"That certainly is some view! I finally admit he does have some facets to him that I've finally found that make sense of the fact that you're going out with him."

"It's not easy, I can tell you that, but then nothing worth fighting for is. I know in my heart that he loves me and cares about me, and that's all that matters."

"So, you know he's the one?"

"I don't know. I know he could be if he's up for the job. Like today, this is a side completely new to me. He's been so sweet and kind, and then he goes and blows up about those damned flowers. Though it is incredibly flattering that he's so into me."

"You guys had a fight about that? Ridiculous." She shook her head. "Well, I figured something would happen, the way you've been wondering about it. Neither he nor you can keep your traps shut. He can't resist blowing steam every few hours, I guess. And you can't help saying everything you feel. A perfect couple."

I rolled my eyes. "Yeah, well, I believe that's a good thing. I'd rather be honest than keep things inside and burst one day. And it's nice to know he feels secure enough with me to blow some steam. As long as he knows where to draw the line and start working on things instead of just steaming about them."

"Wish there was somewhere men could be taught that little piece of wisdom. There's only a few of them out there like that."

I smirked. "Well, I've got one of them, and you can have the next one that comes along."

"I'll drink to that..." She finished the glass. "I'll go get another one."

"Hey! It's close to midnight now. I think you ought
to cut back on those."

"The night is still young, and I have a long way to go... Yo, ho, ho!"

"That's for Christmas, not birthdays." I sighed, smiling, and looked onto the scene below. The city was still lit up like candles in a dark room, and with the moon shining down, everything looked splendid. Closing my eyes, I swayed to the soft music and dreamed of a better tomorrow.

Suddenly, I felt a pull. "There seems to be someone here who wants to dance. "

I smiled contently as Vaibhav pulled me into his arms, careful not to mush the flowers, holding me ever so gently. I opened my eyes and looked at the man who'd come to define my hopes for tomorrow.

"Hi."

"Hi back." He smiled.

We danced to the music, forgetting everything around us as most people in love do, I guess. We didn't talk. There was nothing to be said, but as I rested my head on his shoulder, I knew this was a place I was totally safe.

"Sha?"

"Hmm?" I said, lost in my own world.

"Are you happy?"

"I sure am." I sighed.

"I mean, are you really happy?"

"Well, maybe you'd care to make me a little happier later..." I smiled mischievously.

"A definite affirmative to that."

With that, he twirled me around the hall, with everyone clapping and cheering us on. And then when we stopped, and I was dizzy and delirious, with happiness or the twirls, he shouted, "Everyone! It's almost midnight, and I believe it's time for the birthday cake. "

With my mouth open and my protests unheard, my cherished flowers were taken away from me, and the cake was brought. Laughing, thoroughly embarrassed, I enjoyed everyone singing for me like I was a five-year-old.

My face was already hurting from smiling when everyone around me started singing in funny voices, " For she's a jolly good fellow..."

They clapped their hands thunderously, creating quite a racket.

From behind my parents, I saw V come into the circle. Wondering what atrocities he had planned next, I punched him hard. "What torture are you going to put me through next, you devil?"

He brought out his right hand and handed me the last jewels of the evening, saying, "Torture, my dear, I hope you've found you like enough to endure for the rest of your life."

As he got down on one knee and handed me a rose, I looked around stupefied as everything seemed to go silent around me. Curious, I tilted the envelope to let a ring and a card slide out onto my hand. He grinned and encouraged me with a nod toward the card that I opened to read...

"To a precious joy that brightens my world...
Marry me..."

To this day, my daughters love to hear the story of why I was running around a hall twenty floors above the ground, hitting their father with a bouquet of roses, the day he proposed to me.

THE END

ABOUT THE AUTHOR

Aditi Wardhan Singh is an award-winning, best-selling author. She is an authoritative voice on cultural sensitivity and empowerment, featured on numerous global publications and broadcast networks like NBC, CBS, Huffpost, Thrive, Richmond Family Magazine, Reading with Your Kids podcast etc. Her passion for diversifying dialogue within multicultural families led her to founding the collaborative **RaisingWorldChildren.com** platform. Today, she aims to help parents diversify their libraries by lifting other multicultural authors like herself. In her spare time, she enjoys choreographing dance recitals, volunteering and having impromptu dance parties with her two charming kids.

Her upcoming works include a multicultural children's book about belonging and a unique bilingual Hindi-English resource for children.

Also by Aditi Wardhan Singh

Strong Roots Have No Fear
Raising the Global Mindset

Children's Books

How Our Skin Sparkles
Sparkles of Joy
Sparkles of Joy Activity Book
Small or Tall, We Sparkle After All

www.ingramcontent.com/pod-product-compliance
Lightning Source LLC
Chambersburg PA
CBHW070608310726
48982CB00001B/10
* 9 7 8 1 9 5 6 8 7 0 9 7 8 *